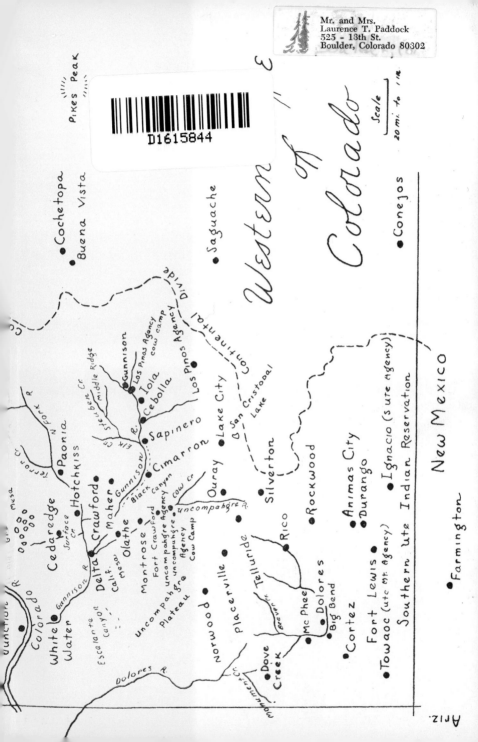

D1615844

Western of Colorado

Scale
20 mi. to 1 in.

Pikes Peak

• Cochetopa
• Buena Vista

• Saguache

• Conejos

Continental Divide

Gunnison
Los Pinos Agency
cow camp
Iola
Cebolla
Los Pinos Agency

Lake City
San Cristobal Lake

New Mexico

Steuben Cr.
middle Ridge
Gunnison R.
Elk Cr.

Sapinero

Cimarron

N Fork R.
Terror Cr.
Paonia
Hotchkiss

Black Canyon
Gunnison
Maher

Ouray

Silverton

Rockwood

Animas City
Durango

Ignacio (S Ute Agency)

Farmington

Grand Mesa
Cedaredge
Surface Cr.
Crawford

Olathe
Calif. Mesa

Fort Crawford
Montrose
Uncompahgre Agency
Uncompahgre Plateau

Uncompahgre R.
Cow Cr.
Cow Camp

Cow Cr.

Uncompahgre Agency
Cow Camp

Telluride
Placerville

Rico

Southern Ute Indian Reservation

Towaoc (Ute Mt Agency)

Fort Lewis

Cortez

White Water

Colorado R.
Gunnison R.

Delta

Escalante Canyon

Norwood

Dolores R.

Beaver Cr.
Mc Phee
Dolores
Big Bend

Dove Creek

Monument Cr.

Junction

Colorado R.

Ariz.

# SUNSET SLOPE

On the Western Slope of Colorado. This typical western Colorado scene was taken in the West Elk Mountains in Gunnison County. *Photo courtesy of Lee Sperry.*

# SUNSET SLOPE

*TRUE EPICS OF WESTERN COLORADO*

*by*

WILSON ROCKWELL

*Jacket and cover design*
*by Velda L. Anglin*

BIG MOUNTAIN PRESS
*Denver*

ACKNOWLEDGMENT

"McCartys' Last Holdup" and "The Escalante Canyon
Duel" are reprinted by permission of the *Empire Magazine*
of *The Denver Post.*

# TABLE OF CONTENTS

# TABLE OF ILLUSTRATIONS

Robert F. Rockwell

# IN MEMORIAM

## *by*

## *Arthur L. Craig*[1]

Since Robert F. Rockwell is somewhat of a western Colorado tradition and since this book was written as a memorial to him, I, an old friend, have been asked to tell you something about him.

I first met Rob during the summer of 1907 when he came to Paonia, Colorado, to visit his aunt, Mrs. R. J. Huff, commonly known as Aunt Ada. Rob was a tall, red-haired, big boned youth with pleasant, Will Rogerian features. He had just recently graduated from the Hill Preparatory School and got in a year at Princeton. In both schools he was a tennis champion. A nasty fall he received when thrown by a runaway horse so impaired his health that he was unable to continue on with his college career. This was a great disappointment to him since he had intended to go through Harvard Law School after graduating from Princeton.

Because he did not respond to medical treatment, doctors thought a good dose of sea air might turn the trick; so his father sent him on a long cruise of the Mediterranean. He wasn't any better when he returned home; so he came out West as a last resort.

Rob's home was Hornellsville, New York, where his father, Mrs. Huff's oldest brother, had one of his big department stores. Rob's uncle, F. R. Rockwell, owned the Paonia Merc. in Paonia. He lived here a while and then moved to Pueblo to accept an attractive promotion as division superintendent of the Denver and Rio Grande Railroad. Mr. Huff, commonly known as "Mick," was managing the Paonia Merc. for Mr. Rockwell when Rob arrived upon the scene.

The former college tennis champion was not to be deprived long of his favorite recreation. News of his presence in the community soon developed the fact that several others were longing for opportunities to keep their game in practice. Among them were capitalist Thomas T. Duffield; Miss Daisy Dixon, principal of the high school; Alonzo A. King, on vacation before his final year in a college of dentistry; L. T. "Ted" Ernst, horticulturist, and myself. A tennis court was roughed out east of the one school building, which now houses the junior high school, and nearly every afternoon its graveled surface showered portions of its poorly manicured inclines to the accompaniment of gentlemanly and ladylike expletives scarcely suitable for the more vigorous sports of the western cattle country.

That the newcomer's tennis was of championship calibre was evident to everybody who observed his distinctive style. Always unhurried, he seemed to have no difficulty whatever in returning his opponents' shots from either side of the court, whether he was playing singles or doubles, and this without any apparent effort.

Interest in tennis in Paonia grew rapidly as more and more of the younger people in the community began playing. Among the recruits were such men prominent in the community as Merle D. Vincent, attorney and politician; postmaster John A. Bunker, and Carrol K. Neilson, another transplanted New Yorker.

Soon after his arrival in Paonia, in 1911, banker M. H. Crissman joined Mr. Vincent and me in installing a private court in Paonia, where Rob was often seen in action.

Rob worked in the Paonia Merc. for a time, but finding confinment of mercantile duties poorly conducive to his physical upbuilding, he purchased a saddle horse and spent hours daily in the saddle. His health began gradually to improve.

One day while riding his horse he encountered Ira J. Nelson, also on horseback, who proposed that Rob accompany him to his cattle ranch on Terror Creek, seven miles north of Paonia. This was the beginning of Rob's interest in the cattle business, and it wasn't long before he purchased seventy-five cattle from Mr. Nelson, arranging to let them be run on the Terror Creek range. That gave Rob his coveted opportunity to ride out into the hills that he came to love so well. But seventy-five constituted hardly a sufficiently large herd to engage his uninterrupted interest, and not many weeks passed before he purchased

225 more cattle, from "Sege" Stratton. As his holdings increased and his interest in the business of cattle-growing grew, his enthusiasm for the occupation prompted him to make a third sizeable investment, and he purchased some 800 cattle which J. H. Kellogg desired to sell.

His own time now overtaxed, Rob employed as foreman a locally prominent cowboy by the name of Jim Thomason—a typical old-time cowpuncher. Much of his success in the cattle business Rob attributed also to the later selections of Tede Hice and Doug Weinant as supervisors of his cattle interests. Tede Hice's son, Glen, once told me an interesting incident about Rob which was very typical of his character.

"Rob Rockwell could handle men smoother than anyone I ever knew," Glen reminisced to me. "When most people bawl a fellow out, it makes him mad, but Rob could call a man down without hurting his feelings and still make him feel like thirty cents.

"I never will forget one time when Rob bought some hay from a fellow who tried to cheat him. I was suspicious that this man was feedin' some of Rob's hay each morning to his own cattle as well as to ours. So, I rode over to this bird's place early one morning and hid behind a hill. I watched him load up his wagon from one of the stacks that Rob had bought. Then he drove his team over to where he was feeding his own cattle and threw out about a quarter of the load before giving what was left to our cattle.

"I told Dad (Rob's foreman) about it; so the next morning he went with me to watch the stealin'. We were

pretty mad about what we seen, and I proposed that we
ride over and tell the bastard what we thought of him.
But Dad said that somebody might get killed, and, besides, he thought that Rob could handle the situation a
lot better than we could. So, we rode like hell to Paonia
to inform the boss about how his hay was being stolen.

"Rob just listened to us with a sort of smile on his
face, and when we got through, he said in that slow, easy
way of his, 'Well, if he needs the hay as bad as that, maybe
we'd better let him have it.'

"We couldn't understand why Rob was so damned
casual about our discovery, and our feelings were pretty
badly hurt. We didn't say anything more about the matter, and neither did Rob. We noticed that whenever Rob
saw the man who was stealing his hay, he was just as nice
to him as ever, and we wondered what the hell!

"When all the hay was fed out, Dad and I happened to
be with Rob when he paid the man off. Rob figured for a
while with his pad and pencil. Then he said, 'Now, let's
see. You sold me one hundred tons at ten dollars a ton.
You have used about a quarter of it to feed your own cattle;
so that leaves seventy-five tons at ten dollars, which totals
$750. Is that right?'

"I really felt sorry for that thief. If ever a man looked
like crawling into a hole, he sure did. He took the check
without saying a word. I don't know of no one else who
could have handled the matter quite as smooth as Rob
did."

Daring, but never reckless, Rob piloted his invest-
ments ever upward and forward. With the growth of his

herds warranting expansion, he sold his interests on Terror Creek and bought one of the district's largest ranches,
originally homesteaded by the true pioneer Samuel B.
Hartman, in portions of Montrose and Gunnison Counties. He and his family spent much of their time at the
ranch headquarters south of the town of Crawford and at
the range camp some fifteen miles farther southward in
the foothills of Black Mesa. Later Rob exchanged the
major acreage for a large apartment house in Denver which
afforded him not only good income, but a home for occu-
pancy during the family's frequent and sometimes extended sojourns in the capital city.

Always an eager student of advanced methods approved
by authorities and his neighbors in the cattle-growing in-
dustry, Rob Rockwell led in the local range-improvement
movement in 1911 by seeding several acres of his range
to various grasses. Even today, with four decades of the
beneficial results of his original test contributing their
influence, our state-sponsored specialists find widespread
adoption of the practice.

The qualities of leadership never are long unrecog-
nized. Rob's progressive methods soon attracted the attention of ever-widening circles, and he was popularly de-
manded for offices in civic and vocational organizations.
It was due to his ambition for the town and the determined
campaign waged by him and his intimate friend, M. H.
Crissman, that Paonia achieved the distinction—which it
held many years—of being the smallest city in the world
with a club of Rotary International. Rob's achievement
was honored by the new club electing him as its first presi-

dent. At home and in widely scattered areas he became much in demand for public appearances as guest speaker at meetings of Rotary.

In addititon to being chosen repeatedly for high offices in stockmen's associations, he was appointed a member of the State Board of Agriculture, which administers the State College of Agriculture and Mechanic Arts at Fort Collins.

During his long tenure of that office he observed the college's growing need of additional facilities for housing its women students. As a result, he devised a plan whereby, with his generous cash contribution, a fund was created for construction of a magnificent dormitory which his colleagues appreciatively named in honor of his late wife, Aileen Rockwell, who died in March, 1938. Through the years "Aileen Rockwell Hall" has become a landmark on the Colorado Aggie Campus.[2]

His health not permitting him to complete his college career, Rob placed a great deal of emphasis on education. He wanted his two sons to go to the same prep school and college that he attended—namely, Hill School and Princeton. When this did not work out, he transferred his wish to his two young grandchildren—Danny and Bobby, who were both two years old at the time of his death. He never lost interest in his alma maters. Each year he sent generous donations, and he followed their athletic schedules with keen enthusiasm. However, he never attended his class reunions at Princeton, feeling that he had not earned the right to do so because he did not graduate. He would have been pleased to know that his college remembered

him with an orange and black wreath, representing the
Princeton colors, at his funeral.

The welfare of youth was ever a major concern of Rob
Rockwell. His willingness to be of constructive service in
the improvement of local conditions for the education and
cultural uplift of young people resulted in his appointment to positions of leadership in such movements. Early
days in the second decade of this century found him active
in promotion of a local Y.M.C.A., and he was a delegate
to the state convention of that institution. He financed
many a promising, underprivileged youth through college.
Some of them became outstanding doctors, scientists and
educators.

To stimulate interest among students in the high
school of the Paonia community, in 1918 Rob and Aileen
established a tradition of awarding valuable trophies to
two members of each successive graduating class. To the
boy leading in scholarship, character, and athletics, and to
the girl standing highest in scholarship, character, and service have gone each year beautiful loving-cups, suitably en-
graved. Recipients of such trophies are selected annually
by a vote of the high school body.

Rob and Aileen also inaugurated the delightful custom
of giving a dinner in their home for the high school seniors
each spring just before graduation.

How thoroughly Rob and Aileen Rockwell became
imbued with the truly democratic spirit of the west was
frequently seen in their homes and at their tables, where
their servants and ranch employees, as well as transient
tradesmen, were treated as members of their family.

Rob, who had been only passively interested in the political career of his friend and tennis associate Attorney Merle Vincent, observed with mild interest that worthy's dilemma as the Progressive Party, with which he had become affiliated under the leadership of Theodore Roosevelt, vanished from the political arena. To the persuasion of his former associates in the Republican Party Mr. Vincent agreed to return to the Republican fold and refrain from seeking political office on condition that he be allowed to name the nominee for State Representative from Delta County in the next election. He then proposed the name of Robert F. Rockwell.

"You know," Mr. Vincent remarked to me, "there's a pretty shrewd young business man, as I have found in handling some of his transactions, notably his purchases of cattle; he will make a splendid office-holder if we can persuade him to make the race."

Rob was persuaded to run, and his excellent record in his freshman term in the State Legislature won him reelection by a handsome majority. At the opening of the session his fellow representatives made him Speaker of the House. Toward the conclusion of that term the public enthusiastically urged his promotion to the State Senate. So little likelihood was there of anyone in the opposite party seriously opposing him, Rob decided campaigning was unnecessary, and he and his family were on an extended visit in the East when the malodorous Nonpartisan League began a surreptitious campaign to unseat him. This attitude on the part of the League was based on an unprecedented collection of unfounded rumors and deliberate misrepresentations, as may be seen from brief reference to a conversation between the campaign manager for a large district of the League and myself.

"You probably know that we hold the balance of power," the official bluffer began, "and we want you to quit supporting Rockwell."

"Why," I asked, "does the Nonpartisan League think it disapproves of Rob Rockwell?"

"Because," the caller explained vehemently, "he's a corporation man."

"Is he?" I asked.

"Sure he is—ain't his father president of the D. & R. G. railroad?"

"No," I answered, "his uncle is general manager of the D. & R. G. railroad, but what would that have to do with Rob's forming an attitude on any political question?"

"Well, his record has been all for big business and against everything that we stand for. If you persist in supporting Rockwell in this next election we'll go down the line and defeat every man Paonia supports."

Then it was my turn to pound the table with my fist in acceptance of his challenge. Not only had I fortified myself with voluminous data concerning the announced objectives and nefarious methods of operation of the Nonpartisan League, but I had only to turn to the published weekly letters Rob had written to the various newspapers to refute every single point the League's district leader had advanced. Widest possible publicity was given to our side of the controversy, with the result that Rob was triumphantly elected to the Senate.

His term of four years had not reached the half-way point when popular sentiment called for his promotion to the Lieutenant-governorship and he was duly installed into that office, although the governorship that year fell into the hands of William E. Sweet, a Democrat.

In reporting a tour of the state before the Paonia Rotary Club, M. H. Crissman, president of the State Bankers' Association at that time, said, "Whenever I told anyone I was from Paonia, he would say, 'Oh, that's where Rob Rockwell lives.' "

It was during one of Governor Sweet's rather frequent absences from Colorado that Republican United States Senator, Sam D. Nicholson, of Leadville, died suddenly. Thereupon, astute but not soo scrupulous leaders in his party whispered to Rob of the tempting opportunity presented to him under such circumstances if he would become a party to a bit of political chicanery. What a delicious chance he had, the tempters suggested, during the governor's absence and his incumbency as Acting Governor, to make a deal whereby he himself could be appointed to the United States Senate! But Rob courageously and steadfastly bade the tempters to begone, and continued on a course forbidding any charge against his personal integrity.

Although the Lieutenant-governorship in Colorado had been considered chiefly a sinecure aside from the duties as presiding officer of the State Senate, Rob proved an active and capable executive, and unwittingly, of course, disclaimed the pronouncement of his namesake younger son, who, when being interrogated for registration as a pupil in the school nearest their temporary home in Denver, was asked his father's occupation. Robert Jr. answered, "He hasn't any."

"What does your father do for a living?" the interrogator asked.

"He doesn't do anything," the young man asserted.

"Surely he does something for an occupation? How does he keep busy?"

"Well, he's Lieutenant Governor," said the lad, "but he doesn't do anything."

Rob's refusal to compromise his principles interrupted a brilliant political career. He was thirty-six years old when he first ran for governor of Colorado. That was in 1924 after he had just completed an outstanding ten-year record as State Representative, Speaker of the House, State Senator, and Lieutenant Governor. He was at that time one of the best known and most popular men in the state and was the most logical Republican contestant for the governorship.

At the Republican state convention in 1924 he received the unanimous designation for the office of Governor, and on that particular year a Republican nomination was the equivalent of an election.

However, politics is never predictable. By a peculiar twist of fate the Ku Klux Klan sprang up shortly after Rob's nomination, and overnight it became the dominant political pressure group in Colorado. One of its members was sent by the organization to see the Republican nominee. He told Rob that the Klan had examined his record and found him to be a suitable candidate. He went on to say that the Klan would support Rob if he would promise not to appoint any Catholics to office during his term as Governor.

Rob fully realized that if he acquiesced to the Klan's wishes in this matter he would have the governorship in the bag. However, unwilling to be tied to a promise he believed unfair, Rob refused to comply with the Klan's ultimatum, even though Rob had no Catholic in mind at the time for an appointment.

The Klan then proceeded to get the required number of signatures to nominate by petition a Klansman to run against Rob in the Republican primary. This man, interestingly enough, was the Klansman who had come to see Rob. The organization also nominated by petition another Klansman on the Republican ticket, who, in order to pick up votes that ordinarily would have gone for Rob, ran as an anti-Klansman.

This astute political chicanery won the election for the Klan's candidate. Out of the several hundred thousand votes which were cast, the Klan's sacrifice candidate, who ran as an anti-Klansman, polled around 2,000. This took enough votes away from Rob to put the Klan's real candidate over by one of the smallest majorities in Colorado's history, thereby temporarily bringing to a close a promising political career.

During my residence of nearly ten years in Greeley and Denver I was deprived of much of the close association with Rob and his family that I had enjoyed when we were neighbors at Paonia, but on returning in response to an unforeseen but attractive call to resume my former occupation at Paonia, it was as if there had been no interruption.

Indeed, from the time of my return it seemed that we were drawn more closely together, partly because of the recent loss of my elder son, Lynn, who was an intimate friend of Rob's elder son, Wilson. The friendship was even more closely cemented by the association during part of Wilson's extended collegiate studies with my younger son, Van, who also is no longer living.

There were, of course, occasional trips to the ranch and the more distant cow-camp, with steak fries, rides, jolly evening conversation around the fireplace, and numerous other periods of enjoyment.

Although he had stoutly maintained that he was through with politics, at least so far as being available for any further public service was concerned, Rob once again entered the political arena in order to occupy his mind after the sudden, untimely death of his wife, Aileen. He was elected to the State Senate and was holding this position of public trust when a delegation of Republican leaders pleaded with him to accept the nomination for United States House of Representatives to fill the unexpired term of the veteran Congressman Edward T. Taylor, a Democrat.

In spite of the frenzied campaign inaugurated by the opposition in a desperate effort to maintain the Democratic Party's power undiminished, Rob was enthusiastically elected in December, 1941. When he went to Washington, he pursued the same plan of keeping his constituents informed as had governed his previous political career, and the reports were generously published by nearly all newspapers in his large district, regardless of political affiliations.

Scarcely had the press wires begun to hum with news of Rob's election to Congress than he brought me a telegram he had received from the political editor of one of the state's largest daily papers.

"This fellow wants me to make statements covering my attitude on a flock of national and world issues," he explained, as I began to read, "and you know I've been concentrating on state and local matters. I can't spare the time to study out the answers he wants, so won't you prepare an outline, point by point, that I can have as a framework on which to build my reply?"

When I delivered the resultant manuscript, which Rob read approvingly, he suggested:

"What do you say we see if Clem can add anything to this?"

Naturally, I assented, and we called at the office of Judge Arthur A. Clements, veteran counselor in both legal and political affairs and staunch friend and supporter of Rob throughout his political career. The judge read no farther than the opening paragraph of the newsman's letter.

"Tell him to go to hell!" he blurted. "Make him understand you're not going to let anybody hogtie you right on the start, even if his paper is all for you."

Twice it was my privilege to accompany Rob Rockwell on extended tours of portions of his congressional district—exceeded in area by only two or three in the United States. The first took us through southwestern Colorado and the second, four years later, to many of the communities of northwestern and central Colorado, where Rob wished to share as many as possible of the acquaintanceships I had formed during my intensive coverage of the mountain states on business visits.

During the campaign between those two tours, when the opposing political party was redoubling its efforts to unseat him, without his knowledge John O. Hovgard, widely known through his executive position in a large coal-producing company and his civic service, and I volunteered to cover a portion of west-central Colorado which Rob's time would not permit him to visit. At one stop a prominent politician asked:

"What's there in it for you two fellows? How come you go out for him unofficially?"

"It's just that we love that man," answered Mr. Hovgard; "we regard him as immeasurably superior to his opposition and, for that matter, to most candidates for other offices, high or low."

As Congressman, Rob had pictures of his ranch employes over the walls of his office in Washington. He idealized these men and would study their letters to him with great interest, often reading them aloud to his close friends. He had little use for people he regarded as "stuffed shirts," regardless of how high their position might be, but he would spend hours visiting and dining with some lonely G.I. from back home who might happen to drop into his office while passing through Washington.

Once a heart-broken kid that he had appointed to Annapolis came into Rob's office after recently flunking his entrance exams. The boy was small, bashful, and quiet. Rob liked his appearance and invited him to his apartment for dinner. That evening he told the youth to study up, and he would appoint him again next year. The boy made the grade next time and later graduated from Annapolis with honors. Like so many young people, he never came near Washington without looking up his friend and benefactor.

Rob never overplayed the power of his financial position. Many a time, in our intimate moments, he either directly or by implication emphasized the fact that he looked upon wealth as a trust to be administered for the benefit of any who were victims of misfortune or otherwise in need. Uncounted are the instances in which he made it possible for a young man or a young woman to pursue a course in higher education or engage in business. Like most of his charities, his profit-sharing with employes was carefully hidden from public view.

One who witnessed the incident tells of the time when an acquaintance long delinquent in liquidating an indebtedness handed Rob a check for fifty dollars. Instead of making a careful entry of the receipt, Rob tore the check into bits and dropped them into a wastebasket.

"What's the idea?" inquired the puzzled one.

"I think you need that money worse than I do," answered Rob. "It's plenty of satisfaction to me to know that I was accommodating an honest man."

Whether among the rough-and-ready characters of the cattle range or suave, polished personalities in financial and governmental circles, Rob Rockwell was a distinguished figure. His ever ready smile and his—unconsciously—princely bearing never failed to attract attention.

This has not been an attempt to enumerate all his excellent qualities, for that is palpably impossible. The nation was made incalculably poorer when the uninformed, unthinking, misguided majority who expressed their choice at the polls in 1948 rudely discarded his accumulated experience, sound judgment, and prestige. Without doubt, although he accepted the result graciously, it hastened the untimely end of his career. He died two years later at his cattle ranch on September 28, 1950.

Shortly after his death, his colleagues in Congress paid tribute to him on the floor of the National House of Representatives. Typical of these remarks was a speech made by a member of the Democratic Party—the Hon. Wayne N. Aspinall:

The SPEAKER. The Chair recognizes the gentleman from Colorado (Mr. Aspinall).

MR. ASPINALL. Mr. Speaker, it is my sorrowful duty to advise the membership of the House of the death of the Honorable Robert F. Rockwell, former Member of this body during the Seventy-seventh, Seventy-eighth, Seventy-ninth, and Eightieth Congresses. He passed away at his home in Paonia, Colorado, on September 28, 1950, at the age of 64 years. Former Congressman Rockwell was born at Cortland, New York, on February 11, 1886, and moved to Western Colorado in 1907, in which State he had been a livestock producer and rancher throughout the many years of his residence there.

Mr. Rockwell gave allegiance to the Republican Party throughout his lifetime and the people of Colorado honored him many times for his upright and conscientious services in their behalf. In 1916 he was elected as the State Representative from his home county of Delta to the State Legislature which position he held for four years. In 1920 he was elected State Senator and served in such capacity until he was elected Lieutenant Governor of Colorado. After his term as Lieutenant Governor, he was defeated for the governorship and a few years later once again elected to the State Senate, which position of public trust he was holding in 1941 when he was elected to Congress from the Fourth Congressional District of the State of Colorado for the seat made vacant in 1941 by the death of the late Honorable Edward T. Taylor, who had been a Member of this body for almost 30 years. Mr. Rockwell held his position in Congress until the first of January 1949.

During his membership in the National Congress, he was a member of the Committee on Public Lands and was serving as chairman of the Subcommittee on Reclamation and Irrigation when he retired from Congress.

In addition to these elective offices, he served for sixteen years by appointment on the Colorado State Board of Agriculture.

Throughout all of his years of residence and office-holding in Colorado, Mr. Rockwell rendered to his community, State and Nation honest and valuable service. He was most conscientious in his political beliefs and in the discharge of the many duties he was called upon to perform. He was at all times a man of a retiring personality, quiet in demeanor and gentlemanly in his associations with his neighbors and colleagues. He was a true conservative in his political philosophy. He never took part in political chicanery, and his own political welfare was of secondary importance in the handling of the affairs of the offices which he held.

During my early years of public service, I became acquainted with this honored and trusted citizen of my State and came to know him as a true and noble character. During the State legislative session of 1941, he served in the position of the minority leader of the State Senate while I held the responsibility of being majority leader. It was a pleasure to work with him. His word was as good as gold. I never knew him to breach a commitment either directly or indirectly. Whenever there was to be a change in policy on the part of him and his associates, he always gave the necessary warning so that the worthwhile services of the two-party system might be prosecuted for the interests of the electorate.

It was my pleasure to not only know him as a political associate but also as a trusted friend in whom I had great confidence. With his passing, he left a record of good neighborliness in his home community, unselfish public service in his State and Nation, and a quiet, generous and understanding relationship with his fellow men seldom surpassed by individuals anywhere.[2]

The tragedy of modern politics is that honest and conscientious public servants are so often unappreciated. However, if the people of this nation are to retain their hardwon liberties against the overwhelming trend toward the welfare state and governmental tyranny, it will be because of statesmen like Robert F. Rockwell, who have the patriotism and unselfishness to sacrifice their own private lives to help preserve the freedom and dignity of the American individual.

[1]The lives of Arthur L. Craig and Robert F. Rockwell had some interesting parallels. Both came to Paonia, Colorado, in the same year. Both were married in the same year, and both had two sons born in identical years. While Rob Rockwell was making a name for himself in politics, Art Craig was going far in the field of journalism. For five years Art was owner and editor of the *Weld County News* in Greeley, Colorado. In 1926 he was elected president of the Colorado Press Association. He was editor of *The Paonian* for about thirty years. As editor of *The Paonian,* he was at one time awarded a trophy by the Colorado Press Association for putting out the best weekly in the state.

Art went through many political campaigns with Rob, and it was he who advised Rob to submit a weekly letter to every newspaper in his district, keeping his constituents fully informed of all of his acts. This was a new idea at the time and was one of the reasons for Rob's many victories in the political arena.

Art's domestic life was very tragic. While his two boys, Lynn and Van, were still small, Art and his wife were divorced. In their early manhood both of his brilliant, handsome sons committed suicide. But in spite of these tremendous adversities and even during the last few years of his life when he was physically incapacitated and nearly penniless, Art always displayed a courage and enthusiasm for life which were his most outstanding characteristics.

Art wrote this article just a short time before he died. He passed away at the Delta Memorial Hospital on May 13, 1954, only four years after the death of the man about whom he writes.

[2]A plaque in the dormitory reads:
"Aileen Rockwell Hall
Home for Women Students
Colorado State College
By Broadening Culture and Forming Lasting Friend-
ships This Memorial Will Be a Worthy Memorial to the
Confidence in Youth Exemplified in the Life of Aileen
Miller Rockwell."

[3]"The Late Honorable Robert F. Rockwell," *Congressional
Record,* Washington, D. C., Dec. 12, 1950, pp. 16625-16626.

# *I*

# DEATH OF AN OUTLAW

Roe Allison, deputy United States marshal, and Jack Bowman, sheriff of Gunnison County, bumped noisily along in a buckboard wagon over the flat, barren adobes toward Morrison's ranch near the present site of Whitewater.[1]

It was April 27, 1882, and the grass and wild flowers, which were beginning to show themselves around the clumps of sagebrush, formed a paradox to snow-capped Grand Mesa looming up in the distance.

Thin cattle of all colors and breeds, which had been driven in from Utah the preceding fall to provide beef for the settlers, paused in their grazing to watch the wagon rattle by.

A few miles farther down the valley a light cloud of smoke was drifting across the clear blue sky, marking the place where the newly born town of Grand Junction was taking root near the junction of the Gunnison and Grand[2] rivers.

This was the first spring in western Colorado after it was opened for settlement, and there existed a striking analogy between the rebirth of nature and the beginnings of civilization on the old Ute Indian reservation.

The two lawmen riding in the buckboard, however, were not thinking about such pleasant comparisons. Their thoughts were centered around the disagreeable and deadly mission immediately ahead of them.

For the past two years a well-organized gang of rustlers had been stealing cattle and horses in eastern Utah and on the Indian reservation in western Colorado. When the reservation was opened for settlement in September, 1881, the gang had continued their raids on the livestock of the incoming settlers.

The leader of this band of outlaws was a colorful individual by the name of George Howard. He was well known by reputation to both Marshal Allison and Sheriff Bowman. Although they had never seen him, they had followed his career and studied his description with such thoroughness that both felt intimately acquainted with him.

George Howard was born in a refined and wealthy home in St. Louis, Missouri. Some of the polish and culture of this early environment apparently rubbed off on him and was never completely lost.

Always restless, he left home while still a youth and started living a rough and pioneer existence in Oregon and northern California. After several years of various and sundry occupations he made quite a strike one season while placer mining on the Columbia River. Selling his gold and claim for a small fortune, he went to San Francisco, where he lived the life of an Epicurean. During this time of bountiful living, he met and married a beautiful girl, who was fascinated by his keen sense of humor, cultured manners, and apparent wealth.[3]

After squandering all of his money and being divorced by his wife, he returned to the frontier and tried to make another stake in Idaho and Washington Territory. He finally drifted into Colorado and had better luck while prospecting at Summitville. Then he followed the rush of prospectors and miners over the range to the rich new mining town of Ouray.

There, in 1876, he got a job driving a stagecoach between Ouray and Salt Lake City for the firm of Meserole and Blake. The route was one of the longest and most dangerous in the West, and George Howard was often commended for his honesty and fearlessness in the performance of his duties.

At one time he was held up by a group of highwaymen in eastern Utah. Although greatly outnumbered, he shot it out with them and managed to get his gold cargo safely to its destination at Salt Lake City. He was not only admired for his steel nerves and cool head, but all the way from Ouray to Salt Lake City people spoke also of his princely manner, ready wit, and pleasing personality.

After carrying the mail for four years, his restless spirit again yearned to break free from the routine and restraints of his job. So he quit driving the stage and started into the cattle business in eastern Utah. To help build up his small herd, he began stealing cattle, and before long became the recognized leader of a gang of cattle rustlers and horse thieves. People who had admired him never could understand the cause for this transformation in his character, but, unable to think of any other reason, many blamed it on the disillusionment of his unhappy marriage.

With cattle and horse stealing becoming a serious problem in western Colorado, Sheriff Bowman of Gunnison County[4] organized a posse, and, with the help of Marshal Allison, set out from the town of Gunnison determined to clean up the rustlers. At Grand Junction the sheriff and marshal received a hot tip that the leader, George Howard, was at Morrison's ranch. So, while members of the posse were running down other clues, the sheriff and marshal had set out for Whitewater.

"Howard has never seen us," Sheriff Bowman said as the officers approached the ranch house; "so if we act like a couple of saw mill operators lookin' for a site, he'll probably never suspect a thing."

"I hope he looks like his descriptions," Marshal Allison remarked, "or we won't know him either."

As the lawmen drove up to the recently built house, a man and woman came forward to greet them.

"My name's Monroe," the man said suspiciously, "and this is my wife. What can we do for you?"

Allison stopped the buckboard by the door of the blacksmith shop and got out. He sized up Monroe quickly but carefully. However, the short, middle-aged rancher did not fit the description of the notorious young outlaw.

"We're lookin' for a sawmill site," Allison answered.
"If Grand Junction grows like I think it will, the town is
gonna need a lot of lumber before long."

"So you want to get in on the ground floor," Monroe
remarked pleasantly, his suspicions fading.

"That's right," Sheriff Bowman interposed, "but we're
new here and don't know the country. I'm from Gunnison
and my friend lives in Denver. Is there any timber around
here?"

"There's quite a little on the other side of the Gunnison, but the river is pretty high right now, and you'll have
to cross at the ford."

While Monroe was pointing out the general location of
the ford, Sheriff Bowman was thinking of some ruse to get
a look inside the ranch house. George Howard might be
in there.

"By the way," he said when Monroe finished speaking,
"would there be any chance of getting a couple of sand-
wiches to take along with us? We didn't bring any grub."

"Sure. I'll have the missus fix yuh up something."

The sheriff followed the rancher into the house while
Allison squatted down in the blacksmith shop door to
await their return.

"This is one of our cow-hands," Monroe said as they
entered the house, introducing Bowman to a medium-sized
man of about thirty-five. He was dressed in the usual cowboy garb of that day and carried the customary six-shooter
on his hip. He was such an average looking person that
Sheriff Bowman jumped to the conclusion that he could
not possibly be the glamorous George Howard.

Although disappointed, Bowman continued with his deception, telling the young man about his search for a sawmill site. The stranger proved to be an easy and interesting person to talk with and produced a map which showed every body of timber and every trail in the region.[5]

"Well, here's your lunch," Mrs. Monroe interrupted finally. "It ain't much but maybe it'll get you through."

The sheriff thanked the woman for her hospitality and walked outside, wanting to get back to Grand Junction as soon as possible and resume the chase.

The young cowboy followed him out to the buckboard. Marshal Allison got to his feet as the two men approached. When the stranger passed the wagon, he glanced at the shotgun and rifle lying under the seat.

"Those guns are a couple of daisies," he said to the marshal, extending his hand in greeting, "I'd like to trade you out of them."

After exchanging a few pleasantries, the attractive newcomer let his hand rest for a moment on the butt of his revolver. The marshal realized that it was an instinctive action, done without any intent to draw the gun. But, nevertheless, Allison suddenly felt his blood run cold. He was not fooled by the ordinary appearance of the cowboy. The marshal's experienced eye immediately recognized him as George Howard, the dangerous, cold-blooded leader of western Colorado's gang of outlaws.

"Well, let's get goin'," Sheriff Bowman said as he walked by the marshal. "We've found out everything that we can here."

Allison nudged the sheriff with his elbow as he passed,

but Bowman, thinking that he had bumped against the marshal's six-shooter, paid no heed to the warning. He was anxious to get back to Grand Junction, feeling that too much time had been wasted already.

The marshal realized that he must act quickly and alone.

"You might tell us again how to find the ford," he said, climbing lazily into the buckboard so as not to arouse Howard's suspicions. Then, he casually picked up his shotgun and placed it on his lap as if preparing to drive off.

"I'll catch my horse and guide you across the river," Howard volunteered unexpectedly. "The ford is hard to find unless you know the country."

"Thanks," Allison replied, suddenly disliking his job as marshal. To arrest such a likeable person sort of went against his grain.

Sheriff Bowman glanced at the marshal in ill-concealed amazement. Why was the marshal continuing to play his little game? Why waste more precious time being guided across the river?

The sheriff was soon enlightened. As the cowboy turned toward the corral to get his horse, the marshal jerked up his shotgun.

"Hands up, Howard!" he ordered.

With the speed of a mountain lion, the concerned outlaw reached for his six-shooter. Before he could shoot, Allison fired, both charges catching Howard in the side as he turned.

Mortally hurt, the cattle rustler started to run, shooting back at the marshal.

Sheriff Bowman, now realizing who the stranger was, grabbed the rifle lying in the wagon and raced around the ranch house to head Howard off.

Allison, amazed that the wounded man did not fall with twelve buckshots in his side, dropped his shotgun and followed Howard with a six-shooter in his hand. The outlaw was displaying the stamina and courage for which he was famous.

When Bowman rounded the east corner of the ranch house, Howard was about one hundred and twenty yards away. In spite of his bleeding side, he was outrunning the marshal.

Bowman pulled up his Winchester and fired. The shot seared through Howard's left shoulder, but he still staggered on, shooting back as he ran.

Holding the rifle up against the building to steady his aim, Bowman shot again. The fugitive pitched forward with a bullet through his head. The checkered career of George Howard was over. He, who had the youth, ability, and opportunity to play an impressive role in developing a new frontier, died an outlaw's death just as western Colorado was beginning to live.

FOOTNOTES

[1]Sidney Jocknick, *Early Days on the Western Slope of Colorado,* The Carson-Harper Co., Denver, Colo., 1913, p. 251.

[2]Now called the Colorado.

[3]*Ouray Times,* May 6, 1882.

[4]At this time Gunnison County included the present counties of Delta, Gunnison, Montrose, Mesa and Garfield.

[5]Jocknick, *op. cit.,* pp. 252-256.

*II*

# THE DISAPPEARANCE OF
# HOWARD CARPENTER

In October, 1921, John Story,[1] an employee of the Anderson sawmill, went deer hunting up the west branch of
Steuben Creek, about fifteen miles north of Sapinero, Colorado. He walked about two-and-a-half miles along the
stream and then turned to his left up a draw on the steep,
heavily timbered mountain side. It was in such gulches
that buck deer often hang out at this time of year.

As he made his way through a narrow opening in the
forest of evergreens, a snowshoe rabbit scampered out of a
nearby bush. Having given up hope of seeing any deer
that day, Story jerked up his rifle and took a shot at the
running target. The bullet missed its mark, and the rabbit disappeared under an old spruce log. Walking over to
the log, the hunter leaned down to move it in order to
frighten the snowshoe out into the open.

As he stooped to grab hold of the log, his body suddenly stiffened. A human skull, half buried in leaves and pine needles, was grinning up at him from beside the log. Quickly regaining his composure, Story picked up his grisly find to examine it more closely. There were two holes in the skull, one at the base and another in the forehead. Whether they were caused by a bullet or by the gnawing of wild animals, Story could not definitely determine.

Other bleached bones of the skeleton were scattered over an area of twenty feet. One lower leg and foot bone, still covered by a shoe, pant leg and sock, all badly deteriorated, lay some distance away from the other remains, evidently having been dragged about by animals.

About five feet up the hill from the bones, the muzzle of a rusted, rotting rifle was sticking into several inches of leaves as if it had been thrown forward many years before and never moved.

Without further investigation the excited hunter picked up the rifle and skull and hurried back to the Anderson sawmill. There he showed his discoveries to W. H. Anderson and James Brewster, and even though night had fallen, the three men started immediately for Cebolla to report the find.[2]

It was October 1, 1911, that thirty-four-year-old Howard Carpenter, a professional guide who lived with his father and brothers at Cebolla on the Gunnison, started out with his party of deer hunters.[3] The group consisted of Terry Owens, chief of the Denver fire department; the Rev. C. F. O'Farrell, big, brilliant Catholic priest of Montrose; Albert Adkins, an employee of Howard Carpenter's father, who went along to help out with the cooking and guiding; and A. M. Paulson and William Snyder, both of Manitou, Colorado.[4] The hunters rode horses belonging to the Carpenters and carried their camping equipment on a string of pack horses.

The day was cool and cloudy as the cavalcade advanced into the mountains toward Steuben Creek—a remote, desolate area far off the beaten trail.

The next day on October 2nd camp was set up, and at noon of the following day, which was Thursday, the party started out on the hunt. They rode about a mile and a half from their camp where they dismounted on what is known as the Middle Ridge, situated between the two branches of Steuben Creek.

Howard Carpenter and Father O'Farrell walked together up the top of the ridge while the others descended the east side of the slope, each taking a different route.

As they strode along the skyline, Carpenter and the priest visited in low tones. Howard told the clergyman that he had never yet failed to get his deer in this region, so far away from the outposts of civilization. They talked casually about other matters, including Howard's future marriage to Anna Landry, a young Montrose girl who was a member of Father O'Farrell's church and who occasionally helped with his housework. Anna planned to leave Montrose in just three more days to meet Carpenter at Cebolla, and they were going on to Denver to be married the next day.[5]

"This little draw here to the west ought to have some

bucks hanging out in it," Carpenter remarked, suddenly changing the subject.

"Then this is where I'm leaving you," the priest said pleasantly. "I hope that you can get along without me."

"I'll try," Howard answered with a smile. "Good luck. I'll see you this evening back at camp."

About an hour after Carpenter and the priest parted company, the muffled boom of a high calibered rifle echoed and re-echoed through the mountain stillness. All of the hunters on both sides of Middle Ridge heard the report and believed that some lucky one of their number had run across a deer. No other shots followed, indicating that the first bullet had found its mark.

Many hours later around four o'clock, another solitary blast once more stirred up the mountain echoes. These were the only shots of the entire day.

By six o'clock all of the hunters had returned to camp except Howard Carpenter, the guide. No one had seen him since the priest left him walking up the ridge. Albert Adkins, Carpenter's assistant, prepared supper while the others visited about the day's hunt.

In questioning each other about the two shots, none of the party admitted firing the first shot which they had heard early in the afternoon. Father O'Farrell said that he was responsible for the second, which had brought down a red-tailed hawk while it was on the wing.

Since no other hunters had been seen in the region, it was assumed that the first shot must have come from Carpenter's gun. Perhaps he had killed a big buck and was somehow being delayed in getting it back to camp.

This was the type of rugged country in the Elk Mountains of Gunnison County where Howard Carpenter was mysteriously murdered. *Photo courtesy of Lee Sperry.*

As the party sat eating their meal, they kept glancing
out into the cold darkness, expecting their guide to ride up
at any minute with his deer. They huddled close to the
fire since the mountain air was getting colder as the evening progressed.

Still too premature to express their uneasiness, the
five men began entertaining thoughts of various mishaps
that might have befallen Carpenter. He might have accidentally shot himself. He might have had a heart attack
or fallen over some precipice. He might even have been
unexpectedly attacked by some old she bear with cubs,
giving Carpenter just one quick shot before she pounced
on him.

All knew that he was too familiar with the country to
get lost in the locality where he was hunting, and if he
had been injured or become suddenly sick, he was the type
of man who had presence of mind to summon help by
firing at least one SOS.

When supper was over, the hunters began voicing their
alarm, and by the light of camp lanterns they returned to
the place on Middle Ridge where the priest said that he
had last seen the guide.

As they continued on up the ridge, the five men at intervals would all shout Howard's name at once and then
stop to listen. But after the Babylonish jargon of the mountain echoes had died away, only the distant murmur of
Steuben Creek disturbed the blanketing silence of the
dark, ominous night.

Finally Adkins, the assistant guide, called a halt to the
futile hunt, and the fearful men returned to camp to wait

for daylight, leading Howard's picketed horse back with them. Unable to sleep because of a nameless dread, they built a bigger fire and remained up all night, discussing Carpenter's fate in low, tense voices.

At daybreak each man gulped down a cup of coffee and once more started out in search of the missing guide. On Middle Ridge they traced the tracks of Carpenter and the priest to the spot where Father O'Farrell had turned westward down the slope. They followed Carpenter's heavy boot prints up the skyline until the marks were lost on rocky ground.

The hunters tried to pick up the trail farther ahead but without success. The guide had apparently swung off the horizon into the heavy timber below, where a thick cushion of pine needles left no tell-tale sign.

The party scattered out and covered the area for miles around, but no further trace of Carpenter could be found. To all appearances, Carpenter had been lifted bodily from the top of the ridge by some monstrous bird and carried away.

Fully realizing by now that something terrible had happened to Carpenter, the group decided that more help was needed and needed fast. There was a possibility that Carpenter was still alive, but if so, he would soon freeze or starve to death in the mountains.

Quickly breaking camp, the hunters hastened to Cebolla, leaving one of their number to bring in the pack train. Upon reaching Cebolla they told J. J. Carpenter, the young man's father, what had happened. Sheriff Pat Hanlon of Gunnison was called, and he immediately organized a

posse from Cebolla, Sapinero, Iola and Gunnison. Early
the next morning—Saturday—fifteen men started out from
Cebolla to renew the search.

Anna Landry collapsed at the telephone when notified
of her sweetheart's weird disappearance. She had made
arrangements to leave Montrose on the next day—Sunday
—to meet Carpenter at Cebolla, and they were to have
gone on to Denver to be married Monday.[6]

After reaching Steuben Creek, the posse followed Carpenter's tracks to where they disappeared on the rocks.
The searchers then examined the ground in ever increasing
circles in desperate but futile efforts to pick up the trail
again.

Word reached Gunnison that more volunteers were
needed. By Monday—the day Howard and Anna had
planned to be married—nearly seventy men were in the
Steuben Creek area. Business in all Gunnison County
towns had come to a standstill with most of their male residents—including merchants, professional men, farmers,
cowboys, and old-time Indian fighters—participating in
the manhunt.

With the chances of finding Carpenter getting better
and better in the vastness and intensity of the search, nature entered the picture to change the normal course of
fate. An untimely blizzard hit Steuben Creek on Tuesday,
covering the ground with four inches of snow.

After the blinding storm, the search was resumed.
Posses passed within only a few yards of the body, but due
to the blanket of snow, the mountains were able to keep
their tragic secret.

Within two weeks most of the riders, exhausted and baffled, had returned home to the daily routine of their respective lives. Only Howard's father, brothers, and a half-dozen relatives and close friends continued the seemingly hopeless search. They remained in the field until late in November when deep snow and sub-zero temperatures forced even this hardy bunch down to civilization.

But with the coming of spring the Carpenters and a few others were back on the job again, pressing the retreating snowline up the creek. They spent a whole month in the area combing it foot by foot, but nature still proved the cleverest and no trace was found of the missing man. Finally, they, too, reluctantly admitted defeat and abandoned the hunt.

Theories and rumors concerning young Carpenter's disappearance ran rampant in the Gunnison region. Since no body could be found, some contended that Carpenter deliberately left the country for reasons of his own, firing his rifle as a last goodbye. Others claimed that some accident must have happened to him and he had frozen or starved to death in the mountains. There were those who thought that some member of his hunting party had accidentally shot him, and many were convinced that he had either been murdered or ended his own life because of certain opposition to his marrying Anna Landry, she being a Catholic and he a Protestant.[7]

As the years passed, Howard Carpenter's disappearance became a legendary story to residents of Gunnison County. Each fall deer hunters passed through the Steuben Creek region, keeping their eyes open for possible revelations.

Howard's father and brothers often visited the area where he had vanished, continually hoping that sooner or later they would find some clue to reveal his fate.

However, it was not until one Saturday afternoon ten years after Carpenter had dropped out of sight that John Story discovered his skeleton about a mile due west of the spot where the guide's tracks had disappeared on Middle Ridge.

When the Carpenter family was notified of the discovery early Sunday morning, they and the sawmill people, accompanied by Acting Coroner C. T. Florer and Undersheriff Lehan, left immediately for Steuben Creek.[8]

In gathering up the scattered bones, they discovered the rotting remnants of several articles of clothing, including boots, hat, and belt. In one small area they ran across a watch, three keys, and some cartridges, all of which J. J. Carpenter recognized as belonging to his son Howard. Shirt buttons, lying face downward in a row, were found, indicating where the dead man had pitched forward and lain before his bones had been dragged about by wild animals.

Earl Carpenter, a brother of Howard, called the coroner's attention to two unusual scars on a tree forty feet up the hill from where the shirt buttons lay.

"Those old scars look like bullet marks to me," he explained.

Coroner Florer examined the scars closely, and then he turned around to look down the 240-foot open lane to where two large spruce trees obscured the view.

While his companaions looked on with interest, Florer

walked down the hill about forty feet to where the buttons indicated that the body had fallen. He hung from an overhanging branch a block of wood about six feet above the buttons. It dangled at a point where he estimated Carpenter's head was at the time he was killed. Then, picking up a rifle, Florer descended the hill two hundred feet to the lower end of the lane. From between the two trees at this place, he aimed his rifle at the block of wood. When fired, the bullet went through the block and lodged in the tree beside the old scars.[9]

"Whoever killed Howard Carpenter stood between those two trees at the foot of the open lane and shot him through the back of the head as Howard was walking up the hill," the coroner testified at the inquest a few days later to Assistant District Attorney Sprigg Shackleford. "In my opinion the bullet which killed Howard made those old scars on that tree there." He pointed toward the marks on the tree, which had been cut down to be used as an exhibit.

The five doctors who testified all stated that the two holes in Carpenter's skull were undoubtedly made by a large calibered bullet which entered at the base of the head and came out the forehead. Because of the enlargement and mutilation of these holes by the gnawing of animals while the skull was green, the doctors were unable to determine the exact caliber of the murder bullet.[10]

After listening to all the testimony, there was only one verdict that the coroner's jury could render—namely, that Howard Carpenter had been shot to death through the head, either feloniously or accidentally, by some person unknown to the jury.

The mountains had finally given up their well-kept secret as to what happened to Howard Carpenter, but the killer still remained unknown. Howard's father hired Samuel D. Crump, a Denver lawyer, to begin an exhaustive investigation.

But the evidence had grown cold in the past ten years, and the clues were meager. The members of the ill-fated hunting party were widely scattered. None of them had been able to appear at the inquest. Terry Owens, former chief of the Denver fire department, had died. Father O'Farrell had been transferred from Montrose to Denver. Albert Adkins had long ago left the region and was thought to be somewhere in Idaho, and neither William Snyder nor A. M. Paulson was readily available.

Anna Landry, Howard's fiancée, had been married for many years and was believed to be in Texas.

The last man of the hunting party presumably to see Howard Carpenter alive also met with a violent death in just a little more than a year after Carpenter's skeleton was found. On January 1, 1923, Father O'Farrell was speeding from a New Year's Day party to perform a wedding at his church in Denver. His car skidded on the icy road into a telephone pole and he was killed.[11]

In 1938 an elderly man from Detroit, Michigan, caused a sensation by confessing that he was the long sought murderer of Howard Carpenter. But after the Gunnison County sheriff brought him to Gunnison, the fantastic confession proved to be a screwball's hoax, concocted to get a free trip to Colorado and to avoid other charges in Michigan.

A fateful snowstorm and ten years of time had covered up the identity and motive of Howard Carpenter's killer. The real story behind the Carpenter case lies forever buried in the silent, desolate mountains of Steuben Creek.

FOOTNOTES

[1]*Denver Post,* Oct. 17, 1921, Selected Scraps on Police Matter, compiled by Sam Howe, Scrap Books No. 38, 39, and 40. In possession of the State Historical Society of Colorado.

[2]Ray Humphries, Chief Investigator, Office of the Denver District Attorney, *Rocky Mountain Empire Magazine,* "Who Killed Howard Carpenter," October 6, 1946.

[3]*Rocky Mountain News,* Oct. 5, 1911, Selected Scraps on Police Matter, compiled by Sam Howe, Book No. 31. In possession of State Historical Society of Colorado.

[4]*Denver Post,* Oct. 17, 1921.

[5]*Rocky Mountain News,* Oct. 5, 1911.

[6]*Rocky Mountain News,* Oct. 5, 1911.

[7]*Denver Post,* Oct. 17, 1921.

[8]Ray Humphries, *op. cit.*

[9]*Ibid.*

[10]*Denver Post,* Oct. 21, 1921.

[11]*Denver Post,* Jan. 1, 1923.

Grand Mesa looking east from Lookout Point. Island Lake in foreground. Ward Lake on the right. Island Lake covers over 500 acres and is the largest lake on the mesa. *Photo courtesy of Benzart, Delta, Colo.*

# III

# THE GRAND MESA FEUD

Grand Mesa, which lies north of Delta and east of Grand Junction, is the largest flat-topped mountain in the world. On this huge, scenic plateau, which averages 10,300 feet above sea level, are more than 200 lakes, many of which are located in ancient volcanic craters. Grand Mesa has become one of the most widely known playgrounds of Colorado with its fishing, boating, hunting, and horseback riding. Its development as a resort constitutes one of the most exciting chapters of Western Colorado history.

In the early 80's William Alexander came to Grand Mesa and took up a 160-acre preemption right near a body of water now known as Alexander Lake.[1] He lived there ten years and then mysteriously disappeared. During his stay on Grand Mesa he took into partnership Richard Forrest, and Forrest Lake was later named in honor of him.

Alexander and Forrest constructed a hotel and fish

hatchery near Alexander Lake, and in 1884 the partners began constructing dams and developing the lakes in the vicinity of their claim for fishing and raising trout.[2] The lakes which they improved became known as the Alexander group and included Alexander, Barren, Island, Forrest, and Ward Lakes.

In 1886 the Surface Creek Ditch and Reservoir Company contracted with Alexander and Forrest to assist the company in locating and constructing dams in lakes and sloughs on Grand Mesa for the Surface Creek irrigation system. In return for their help, the company gave the two men fishing privileges. However, the stockholders of the company retained the right to fish in the lakes.

Alexander and Forrest went ahead with their business of propagating and selling fish, but they allowed the public to fish in their lakes without any restrictions. When Alexander disappeared, Forrest succeeded to all of his partner's rights and continued the old policy of unrestricted fishing. Then, around 1896 Richard Forrest sold his 160 acres of land and his fishing rights to William Radcliffe, an Englishman.[3]

As soon as Radcliffe obtained title to Forrest's rights, he immediately sought to exclude the public from fishing in his lakes without a permit. The public resented the Englishman's change of policy. The stockholders of the Surface Creek Ditch and Reservoir Company, in particular, were antagonistic since they considered their fishing rights equal to Radcliffe's.

Others had fishing rights in lakes outside Radcliffe's jurisdiction. In the 80's S. L. Cockreham had established a

160-acre claim, which included a portion of the Eggleston, Barren and Alexander Lakes. About 1890, fifteen men purchased the Cockreham claim for their own recreation. This group called themselves the Grand Mesa Resort Company, which is still in existence. This was the beginning of Grand Mesa's development as a summer resort.

Radcliffe was supported by both the Forest Service and the Fish and Game Department in his feud with the residents of Surface Creek Mesa and Delta. With the help of a law passed by the state legislature in 1899 which gave to individuals the right to lease public lakes, the Englishman obtained a lease to the Alexander group of lakes for $145 which permitted him to sell fish and exclude the public from his premises. Until this law was passed, his right to the lakes was primarily a moral one. Radcliffe gave the state a few trout spawn and seined several thousand pounds out of the lake each year, which he sold for thirty-five cents a pound.

In spite of Radcliffe's opposition, the public continued to fish in his lakes as they had before. As a result, Radcliffe hired a number of guards, all of whom were deputized as game wardens under the State Fish and Game Commission. Feeling against Radcliffe ran higher than ever at this show of force.

On Sunday afternoon of July 14, 1901, W. A. Womack, Frank Hinchman, Dan and Jack Gipe and Frank Trickle, ranchmen of Surface Creek Mesa, were riding in the vicinity of Island Lake, one of the Alexander group belonging to Radcliffe.[4]

"Let's go over to Island Lake and catch a few trout," Frank Trickle suggested.

"It's all right with me, but the Englishman won't like it," Dan Gipe said.

"Here comes one of his game wardens now," Frank Hinchman remarked as Frank Mahoney appeared.

"Good afternoon," the deputy game warden greeted as he rode up to the group.

The ranchers made no reply as they jogged along the trail.

Sensing the unfriendly feeling toward him, Mahoney instantly assumed a belligerent attitude.

"You are on private property," he warned, "and no one can fish in the lakes here without a permit."

"You can't stop us from fishing here," Womack spoke up. "I'm one of the largest stockholders in the Surface Creek Ditch and Reservoir Company which helped to build up these lakes. We have fishing privileges here which are just as good as Radcliffe's."

"I have my orders," Mahoney snarled, "and I won't let you fish here—fishing privileges or no fishing privileges."

With this threat Mahoney rode away, and the others continued on to Island Lake. Mahoney was there awaiting them. He was in an ugly mood.

"This is my last warning," he said. "You can't fish in the lakes!"

"If you doubt my right to fish here," Womack said, "go ahead and arrest me. We'll let the courts decide who's right."

GRAND MESA HOTEL

An angry mob of 100 armed men burned the Grand Mesa hotel, shown above, to the ground while they awaited the arrival of the owner, William Radcliffe, an Englishman. The mob violence was provoked by the shooting of W. A. Womack, a fisherman, by Frank Mahoney, a deputy gamewarden hired by Radcliffe to prevent fishing in the Grand Mesa lakes. This picture was taken in 1894. *Photo courtesy of Ernest Dixon.*

Mahoney's face turned red with anger as he reined his horse away. He intended to get reinforcements and return.

Then, he thought he heard one of the fishermen laugh. He wasn't sure, but it sounded as if the group were making fun of him.

This was too much for the hot-headed game warden. Completely losing his head, Mahoney whirled his horse around and whipped out a revolver.

Without aiming, he turned the gun on Womack and pulled the trigger. Surprised at the warden's action, the Surface Creek rancher jumped off his horse and tried to hold the animal between him and Mahoney as a shield.

The berserk game warden then took a shot at Frank Hinchman, whose mount was standing in the shallow water of the lake. The slug hit Hinchman in the leg, and he spurred his horse out of range.

Womack's horse, frightened by the shots, turned and faced the gunman, leaving Womack exposed. Mahoney, who was only about twenty-five feet away from the defenseless man, emptied his gun at him. One of the bullets went through Womack's leg, and another lodged in his chest.

As Womack fell, Mahoney turned to the others and shouted, "You damned sons of bitches, get out of here or I'll kill every last one of you!"

His temper suddenly cooled as he saw blood oozing from the fallen man's chest. Womack did not move as he lay there beside the lake.

Fear replaced rage as it gradually dawned on the impulsive Mahoney that he had killed a man.

"Just a minute!" he called suddenly to the departing

horsemen. "One of you ride to Delta and get the sheriff. The rest of you can come back and take care of your dead."

Mrs. Womack and her daughters were camped about two miles away, and they were informed of the shooting as quickly as possible. They rode to the dying man as fast as they could.

Doctor Hick and Doctor Miller of Delta left for the Mesa as soon as the news reached them by telephone from Cedaredge, but Womack died about ten o'clock that night before they arrived.

The family of the game warden occupied a cabin across the lake from where the shooting occurred, and the killer with his wife and children and the other game wardens, fearful of the public's reaction, sat out in front of the cabin until about three o'clock the following morning. They were well-armed and kept a big camp fire burning all night so that a party of lynchers could not surprise them in the darkness.

Afraid and conscience-stricken, Mahoney finally started for Delta on horseback by a round-about trail. Shortly thereafter twenty-five men from Surface Creek arrived at the warden's house, looking for him. When Mahoney rode into Delta around eight o'clock that morning he immediately gave himself up to Sheriff George Smith. The sheriff turned his prisoner over to his deputies, Tom Smith and Charles Owens, and, accompanied by Coroner S. B. Houts and District Attorney Millard Fairlamb, left at once to investigate the killing.

The murderer was placed under a strong guard, and it was feared all day Monday that some effort to lynch him

would be made by the incensed people of Delta and Surface Creek. During the day he was kept in the jury room of
the Delta court house. Horsemen kept arriving in town
during that evening, and the deputies, fearing a raid, decided to smuggle their prisoner out of the jury room and
hide him.

At eight o'clock while a case was being tried in the
county court room, Deputy Owens, unobserved, took his
prisoner downstairs and out a back door where a team
awaited them in the alley. The driver cracked his whip,
and the team sped to the Smith ranch about two miles distant up the Uncompahgre River, where Mahoney was hidden until the next morning.

The county court finally adjourned at 12:30 A.M., and
after everyone had departed, a mob of about 150 armed
men smashed into the court house. They broke in every
door of the building in search of the prisoner. Failing to
find him, they visited the jail and every place in town
where they thought he might be hiding. The intensive
search was continued until four o'clock Tuesday morning
by the avenging mob.

At daybreak the deputy sheriff returned to Delta with
the game warden. About ten o'clock the two deputies drove
to Olathe with the prisoner and caught the east bound
train for Gunnison.

That night about one hundred armed men rode to
Alexander Lake from Surface Creek and ordered all of
Radcliffe's men to leave by morning and to take their belongings with them. Fortunately for the Englishman, he
was away at the time. After the hired help and their fam-

ilies had gone, the mob set fire to Radcliffe's hotel and cabins. The fish hatchery, boats and nets, which did not exclusively belong to the Englishman, were left unmolested.

A short time after the killing, word got around that Radcliffe was on his way back to the lakes. Another mob gathered there. While waiting for their victim, they set fire to all the remaining property that had been spared, except for the ice house, which would not burn.[5]

Judge Alfred R. King of Delta, who was on his way to Denver on the train, unexpectedly met Radcliffe in Montrose during a pause at the station. The Englishman was returning to his resort as rumored. King tipped him off about the "reception committee" and advised him to stay away.[6]

Radcliffe took the judge's advice and turned back, never again to return to western Colorado. He organized the Grand Mesa Lake and Park Company and conveyed his rights to this company of which he was the principal stockholder. After that he leased the lakes to the Federal Bureau of Fisheries, which was more successful than the Englishman in excluding fishermen. A number of men who persisted in fishing in the lake without a permit were indicted and prosecuted by a U. S. Attorney. They finally were allowed to go free after promising not to repeat the offense.

Mahoney, the deputy game warden who killed Womack, was tried in Gunnison. He was convicted of voluntary manslaughter and sentenced to eight years in the state penitentiary.[7]

The Grand Mesa Resort Company, composed of Delta

residents who in the 1890's had acquired the S. L. Cock-reham claim, continued to oppose the bureau's fishing restrictions. Finally, about 1911, this resort company purchased the interests of Radcliffe and his associates, receiving title to all of his property on Grand Mesa. Soon after this the resort company incorporated. The original members took out stock in the company and sold stock at fifty dollars a share to obtain funds. They tried to sell shares in Montrose, Grand Junction, and other neighboring towns but with little success. The vast majority of shares were sold to Delta County people.

From the money obtained, the Grand Mesa Resort Company built a fish hatchery, restocked the lakes, and improved the road from Cedaredge. This road was further improved by the State Highway Department in 1923 and 1924.

As soon as the Grand Mesa Resort Company obtained Radcliffe's fishing rights in 1911, the Grand Mesa lakes were opened to the public. The company has kept the lakes stocked throughout the years and has never exercised its rights to sell fish. The Fish and Game Department is allowed to take all of the eggs and spawn in return for restocking the lakes each year.

The English ambassador used his influence to get the United States government to reimburse Radcliffe $25,000 for the damage done to an English subject. Theodore Roosevelt was President of the United States at this time.

On May 10, 1938, William Radcliffe died in Kent, England, at the age of eighty-one.[8] He was an expert on fishing, having traveled extensively during his lifetime to study the folklore of fishing. He was a fine gentleman, his difficulties on Grand Mesa resulting entirely from his inability to understand the people of Delta County and their inability to understand him.

FOOTNOTES

[1]Harry A. Cobbett, Interview, 1952.
[2]J. C. Hart, CWA Interviews, 1933-34, Delta Co., p. 60.
[3]*Delta Independent,* August 24, 1937.
[4]*Delta Independent,* July 19, 1901.
[5]Milton R. Welch, "Grand Mesa History," *Delta Independent,* August 24, 1937.
[6]Ula King Fairfield, *Pioneer Lawyer,* W. H. Kistler Stationery Co., Denver, Colo., 1946, p. 71.
[7]Welch, *op. cit.*
[8]Fairfield, *op. cit.,* p. 73.

Delta's Main Street as it looked at time of bank robbery. *Photo courtesy of Elmer Skinner.*

## IV

# THE McCARTYS' LAST HOLDUP

On the morning of September 7, 1893, three men on blooded horses rode southward up the alley between Main and Meeker Streets in the town of Delta, Colorado. Upon reaching the rear of the Farmers and Merchants Bank the horsemen stopped and dismounted. One of them held the horses while the other two walked up a narrow board sidewalk, which led around the north side of the bank building to Main Street.[1]

As soon as his companions had disappeared, the man holding the horses pulled a whiskey bottle from his pocket and took a long swig from it. He was about thirty-five years old, short, with a dark mustache and three weeks growth of beard. He wore a gray sack coat, white hat with a leather band, and overalls.

When the other two men reached Main Street, they turned and walked to the open door of the Farmers and

Merchants Bank. As they entered, one of them quietly closed and locked the door.

It was a little after ten and the bank had just opened. The safe was ajar, and paper money and coins had been placed on the counter in position for the day's business. A. T. Blachly, the cashier and co-founder of the bank, was typing, and H. H. Wolbert, the assistant cashier, was working at his desk.

As the strangers approached the cashier's window, Blachly got up to wait on them.

"This is a holdup," one of them ordered, suddenly pulling out a six-shooter. "Put up your hands and keep still!"[2]

Startled, Blachly and Wolbert slowly raised their hands.

"You can't get away with this!" Blachly exclaimed.

The bandit who had him covered waved his gun menacingly. "Shut up and be quiet if you want to live," he warned.

The man who spoke was a short, medium-sized, beardless youth of about twenty. He was dressed in a dark coat, blue overalls, and low-cut shoes. He was not tanned, and his hands were soft and white as if accustomed to indoor work. There was an insolent, arrogant expression on his pale face, which should have warned Blachly that he meant business.

His companion was a short, husky, villainous-looking man of about forty. He had a sandy mustache, straggly beard, and several weeks growth of whiskers.

The youthful bandit started to climb over the partition, giving Wolbert a chance to reach for his revolver.

"Drop that gun!" the older bandit snapped, "and walk around to the window!"

As the young bank robber appeared over the partition, Blachly shouted for help in a great, sudden voice. The boy bandit fired twice, one of the bullets hitting Blachly in the top of the head, killing him instantly, and the other bullet thudding harmlessly into the floor.

The scream and gun reports were heard all over Main Street, sounding the alarm. Welland Jeffers, a boy who lived with his mother in the back of her millinery store a block away, heard the shots and thought that someone was shooting at his pigeons in the alley. Others, closer to the scene, realized instantly that the bank was being held up, and Main Street was quickly alive with activity.

These unexpected events disrupted the bank robbers' plans. In the young bandit's overalls a large sack was found later, which he apparently had intended to fill methodically with money from the counter and open safe. However, with armed men running toward the bank from all directions, he merely had time to snatch a few handfuls of bills and coins from the cashier's desk and stuff them into his pockets. Then, grabbing a bag of gold from the safe, he and his associate left hastily by the rear door, escorting the assistant cashier along with them.

Upon entering the alley, they discovered their accomplice standing there with his six-shooter pointed at W. R. Robertson, a Delta attorney, who had his hands in the air. Robertson had been in his office in the back portion of the bank building when Blachly was killed, and he had rushed

A. T. Blachly yelled a warning.  Fred McCarty shot him down.

Mary Blachly, wife of the slain cashier, raised her eight sons.

out the back door, where he encountered the third bandit holding the horses.

The three men hurriedly mounted their hot-blooded horses and galloped northward down the alley in the direction they had come, leaving, in their haste, the bag of gold behind them on the ground.

Ray Simpson was in his hardware store directly across the street from the bank, cleaning his .44 caliber Sharps rifle at the time of the holdup. He was a tall, slender, well-dressed man of thirty-one. He was so quiet and unassuming that few Delta residents suspected what a great sportsman and crack shot he actually was. Even as a boy in his native state of Kentucky, he did a lot of squirrel hunting and, as a result, learned to shoot a rifle accurately from the hip without putting the gun to his shoulder. He had an unexcitable disposition and was the type of man who could calmly hold his fire until the last instant while being charged by a bear or lion.[3]

Hearing the cry of terror and the shots, Ray Simpson quickly loaded his gun and ran over to the corner of Third and Main and continued on up Third Street to the alley, where the bandits were making their get-away.

The horsemen were about half a block away and moving at full speed when Simpson arrived. The clatter of their horses' hoofs could be heard above the commotion on Main Street. Simpson jerked up his Sharps rifle and shot from the hip without taking aim. The rear bandit, later identified as the older man who had entered the bank, fell headlong from his running horse with the top of his head blown off. His young companion, who had shot the cashier,

Ray Simpson emptied two McCarty saddles with his rifle; was haunted by outlaw's letters.

was riding just ahead. He looked back at the fallen rider
and started to pull up his horse. Then, seeing that his
comrade was past help, he dug his heels into his horse's
sides and raced on.

Ray Simpson was not a natural killer, and he started
to lower his rifle.

"Give it to 'em, Ray!" one of the spectators cried.

The two escaping bank robbers were nearly a block
away when Simpson fired again, but miraculously the second bullet found its mark in the young bandit's head, and
he fell sprawling into the alley, money scattering in all
directions from his bulging pockets.

A third shot from Simpson's gun went wild, striking
one of the riderless horses in the side. The wounded horse
clattered back to Third Street, where he bled to death.
The other riderless horse, covered with blood from his
dead rider, also galloped back across Third Street, where
Miss Inez Olmsted, a plucky young Delta woman, caught
and tied him.

Simpson took one last shot at the remaining bandit,
just as he turned his fast-moving, blaze-faced bay down
Second Street. The horseman thundered into Main Street
and pounded northward over the Gunnison River bridge
toward Grand Junction.[4]

Sheriff Bill Girardet was sitting in the *Delta Independent* newspaper office a block away at the corner of Fourth
and Main when the shooting occurred. He quickly mounted his horse and was giving chase, accompanied by Newt
Castle, F. W. Childs, I. N. McMurray, Mark W. Brown,
Walter Wagner and the marksman, Ray Simpson. This

posse chased the bandit all the way to Grand Junction, but he had the fastest horse and made his escape. A $500 reward was offered for his capture, dead or alive, but he was never caught.

When Ray Simpson returned from the chase, his beautiful southern wife met him as he walked up Main Street still carrying his rifle. She put her arms around him and began to cry.

"Now, honey," he said, calmly puffing on a cigar, "there's nothing to get excited about."

The two dead bank robbers were propped up against a barn and F. M. Laycock, Delta's first photographer, took their pictures, putting the older man's hat on in order to conceal the gaping wound in the top of his head. These pictures were sent to the state penitentiary and elsewhere for identification purposes.

The next day after the robbery, the bodies of the bandits were placed in one box and buried in the Potter's Field Cemetery at Delta.

Relatives later identified the older bank robber as Bill McCarty of Utah, and the younger one as his son, Fred. It has always been assumed that the escaped bandit was Tom McCarty, brother and uncle of the dead men.[5]

A. T. Blachly, the cashier who was killed, left a widow and eight young sons. Mary Blachly, his widow, was a cultured, college-trained woman. She gave music lessons and played the organ at church in order to support her large family. She sent them all through college, and every one made a mark for himself in his respective community.[6]

Soon after the robbery Ray Simpson, the hero of the

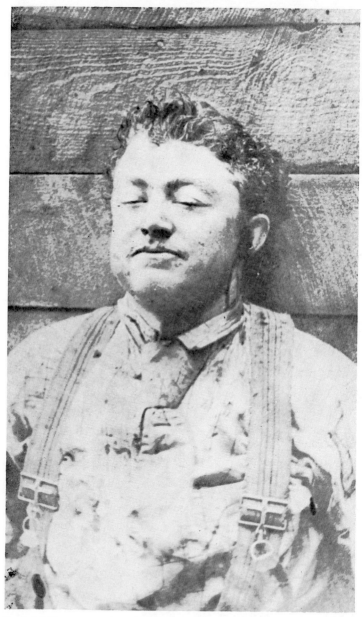

Fred McCarty, son of Bill McCarty, was the killer of A. T. Blachly, cashier of the Farmers and Merchants Bank of Delta. He was killed by Ray Simpson on Sept. 7, 1893, as he and two other robbers attempted to escape.

Bill McCarty, father of Fred McCarty, helped his son hold up the Farmers and Merchants Bank. Bill McCarty was the first bandit to fall from his horse when Ray Simpson began shooting. The third outlaw made his escape.

day, began receiving letters from the escaped bandit,
threatening Simpson and his wife and daughter.[7]  The menacing notes kept coming in month after month, continually preying on his nerves.  Simpson kept a loaded gun near
him both night and day.  His wife finally had a nervous
collapse; so he eventually left Delta to get away from the
avenging bank robber whom he could not forget.  Simpson
died in California in 1940 at the age of 78, and was buried
in the Forest Lawn Cemetery at Glendale.[8]

    September 7, 1893 was a long day in Delta.  For some
it proved to be an eternity.[9]


FOOTNOTES

    [1]*Delta Independent,* September 8, 1893.

    [2]Coroner's inquest papers, written September 7, 1893, filed
in district court at Delta Feb. 12, 1894.

    [3]Interview with J. W. Smith, a pioneer of Delta, 1952.

    [4]Ben Laycock, twelve-year old son of F. M. Laycock who
took pictures of the dead bandits, disagrees with the account
in the *Delta Independent.*  He, an eyewitness, states that as
soon as Fred McCarty shot Blachly the bandit holding the
horses tied his companions' horses and galloped away before
his accomplices came out of the bank.

    [5]J. W. Smith, interview.

    [6]Ula King Fairfield, *Pioneer Lawyer,* W. H. Kistler Sta-
tionery Co., Denver, Colo., 1946, p. 68.

    [7]Simpson had two more daughters after leaving Delta.

    [8]Fairfield, *op. cit.,* p. 66.

    [9]Tom McCarty—the escaped bandit—is believed to have
helped rob the San Miguel Bank at Telluride four years before on June 24, 1889.  That morning three horsemen rode

up in front of the bank. One sat on his horse and held his companions' horses while the other two entered the bank and held up C. L. Hyde, the assistant cashier. Backing out with all of the money in sight, they mounted their horses and galloped west on Main Street. Sheriff J. A. Beattie organized a posse and started after the bank robbers who had a big lead. Somewhere between the towns of Rico and Dolores the bandits changed mounts, driving the first relay of horses ahead of them. They left behind a big bay horse of Tom McCarty's since it was too winded after the long ride to keep up. All of the bandits escaped, but Sheriff Beattie got Tom McCartys' horse and rode him around Telluride for years afterwards. (L. G. Denison, "Tales of an Early Pioneer," *Telluride Journal,* Jan. 14, 1938.)

J. W. Hugus and Co. store at time of robbery.

# *V*

# THE MEEKER BANK ROBBERY

It was a crisp, colorful afternoon on October 13, 1896, when three horsemen splashed their spirited mounts across White River just south of Meeker, Colorado. Struggling up the bank, the rangy, smooth-limbed horses entered a grove of old cottonwoods, which extended to the outskirts of the small cowtown. Emerging from the trees, the triumvirate rode up to the rear of the big Hugus & Company general store and dismounted. They tied their horses to some empty freight wagons, which had recently hauled in goods from Rawlins, Wyoming, and strode up the board sidewalk to the rear side entrance of the widely known store.[1]

One of the three—Jim Shirley—walked with a slight limp, and he looked much more at home in the saddle than on the ground. He was a pleasant-faced, medium-sized man of about forty-five. Blue goggles, which helped disguise his face, covered deep-set, bluish gray eyes. The collar of a black sweater was pulled up around his chin, which was covered with a three-weeks growth of dark beard.[2]

"I'll meet you inside," Shirley said, stopping by the rear door. "Good luck."

He did not enter immediately but watched his two companions round the corner of Sixth and Main in the direction of the front door.

At this time the Bank of Meeker was partitioned off in the east front portion of Hugus & Company, and it was managed by the same clerical force that did the bookkeeping for the store. A. C. Moulton, store manager, was also cashier of the bank.[3]

It was right on three o'clock when the two strangers appeared at the front entrance. The older man, who was later identified as George Law, turned to the left and walked up to the cashier's window. He was a powerfully built, reddish-haired man with a light sandy moustache. His younger comrade, whose identity was never discovered, proceeded down the right aisle toward the center of the store. He was in his early twenties and had a large, clean-shaven face and a thick, bull-like neck. Long dark hair showed from under his hat brim. His companions called him The Kid.

Simultaneously with the entrance of George Law and The Kid, Jim Shirley limped unobserved through the rear door.

As the three men entered, Mr. Moulton, the store manager, and his clerks were busily engaged waiting on several customers. David Smith, the assistant cashier, was taking a deposit from Joe Rooney, a clerk at the Meeker Hotel.

George Law waited patiently until the assistant cashier had finished his transaction with Rooney. Then the big newcomer stepped quickly up to the cashier's cage. Suddenly exhibiting a six-shooter which he poked through the brass bars of the window, he fired close to the head of Smith, who was writing down his entry.

"Throw up your hands," the gunman ordered as Smith glanced up in bewilderment.

Smith was slow in complying; so once more the trigger-happy bandit blazed away.

This is certainly no professional job, Smith surmised as he slowly raised his arms. Those two shots will rouse the whole town.

At the sound of the loud reports, the clerks and customers paused in their dealings to look about. As they did so, Jim Shirley and The Kid pulled six-shooters from their holsters and soon had the half-dozen men in the store corraled near the center of the room with their hands in the air.

Law's gunplay attracted the attention of Tom Sherrin of the Meeker Hotel, C. J. Duffy, Phil Barnhart, and a few others who happened to be within hearing range of the blasts. These men ran up the streets spreading news of the robbery, and minutes later residents of the village were running for their guns. Armed men started appearing at doors, windows, and behind buildings, waiting to greet the bank robbers when they came out of the store.

Apparently amateurs at the business, the bandits didn't fully realize how quickly their time was running out. After George Law's ill-advised and fateful two shots, each minute of delay in making a get-away helped seal their doom.

While keeping Joe Rooney and the assistant cashier covered, Law moved around to the door of the bank office and tried to force it open. Unable to do so, the flustered gunman marched Rooney and the assistant cashier down the aisle to where the others were standing in the middle of the store.

Jim Shirley, the ringleader, then took over. He stumped up to the widely-known manager of the store and remarked pleasantly, "Mr. Cashier, we want you!"

He directed Moulton politely to the locked door of the bank office. Law followed while The Kid was left in sole charge of the prisoners.

"Unlock the door," Shirley ordered upon reaching the bank office.

The manager glanced at the quiet, steely eyes behind the blue goggles and didn't hesitate.

"Where is your money?" the soft voice continued.

"There it is," Moulton replied, nodding toward the cash drawer which was part way open. "Help yourself."

Shirley's calm, efficient manner helped steady his jittery, red-headed accomplice, who pulled an old sugar sack from a pocket and dumped the contents of the drawer into it. Then all four returned to the center of the store, where the prisoners were watching fearfully with their tired arms still held high.

Time had not quite run out for the bank robbers, and

they still had an even chance of making their escape in spite of the two blundering shots at the start of the holdup. However, Shirley, apparently bent on carrying out his previous plans to the letter, took another fatal five minutes to secure all of the rifles and ammunition in the store. He filled the magazines of three and broke the stocks of the others.

Having methodically completed this task, he handed two loaded Winchesters to his partners and kept the other for himself. At long last, the robbers with their captives finally started filing out the rear door into the cool autumn sunshine. First came the leader, Jim Shirley, pushing Joe Rooney ahead of him as a shield. The Kid and George Law followed with Moulton, Smith, Booth, W. P. Herrick, Victor Dikeman and several other hostages.

The street was deserted, and the air was heavy with a portentous silence, broken only by the occasional chirping of sparrows. The little group, however, was not fooled by the empty appearance of the town. Each man knew that their progress was being watched by an army of hidden marksmen who were biding their time, waiting for an opportunity to shoot without endangering the hostages.

Suddenly Jim Shirley spied one of the townspeople peering from behind the grain warehouse of Hugus & Company. He jerked up his Winchester and fired, the echoing report momentarily shattering the ominous stillness. N. H. Clark ducked back into hiding with a bullet in his chest.

The unusual procession continued on for about thirty more feet to where the bandits' horses were tied. Jim

Shirley and George Law started to untie them while The Kid kept guard.

Shirley smiled as he reached for his bridle reins. The worst seemed to be over. There was still a gauntlet of gunfire to gallop through as soon as the hostages were released, but after he and his colleagues were once in the saddles, it wouldn't take their fast horses long to reach the protection of the nearby cottonwoods, and speeding targets were hard to hit.

Besides, Shirley had a surprise in store for the Meeker residents. He was depending on this trump card to pull him out of the hole. The townspeople would be expecting the bank robbers to strike north for the open country and undoubtedly had stationed their sharpshooters and posse accordingly. They didn't know that the three horsemen had cut the fences and gates in the opposite direction just before they crossed the river into town. In making the surprise get-away, the bank robbers intended to back-track southward through the cut fences and then circle north to where a relay of horses awaited them at their camp on the head of Three Mile Gulch, eight miles above town.[4]

Before Shirley had a chance to play his trump, something went wrong—something that he had never taken into consideration. One of the prisoners, ignoring The Kid's threatening rifle, unexpectedly let his tired arms fall to his side and ran like a scared rabbit for shelter. His aching shoulders had finally become too exhausted to keep his arms up any longer.

Shirley dropped his reins and reached for his Winchester, but before he could grab the rifle, the other prisoners scattered in all directions, like so many mice.

The Kid, taken completely by surprise, sent the bullets flying thick and fast for a few seconds. Victor Dikeman was hit in the right arm. Booth received a wound in his left arm, and W. P. Herrick had his finger nicked by a passing slug.

The scampering hostages were barely out of the line of fire when the waiting townspeople went into action. Five bullets instantly found their mark in The Kid's body, one of them penetrating his heart. He spun around and fell on his back with his young face turned upward toward the sky.[5]

Shirley went down with a bullet through his left lung. Game to the last, he whipped out his six-shooter, and though unable to regain his feet, he sprayed lead in all directions until he died.

Seeing his pals drop in the sudden cataclysm, George Law, confused and panic-stricken, dropped his bridle reins and sprinted toward the river. A bullet through his right lung and another in his left leg brought him down.

Before he died an hour later, he gave, in response to numerous questions, ficticious names of himself and partners.[6] In his last, barely audible utterance he whispered the single word, "Mother!"

Seventeen days after the attempted robbery, Sam Wear of Meeker ran across the camp of the dead bank robbers at the head of Three Mile Gulch, a tributary of Strawberry. There he found the three relay horses, three rifles, and bedding. The horses had been without feed and water for

Jim Shirley near wagon wheels; "The Kid" in front of tree.

George Law—last of the bank robbers to be shot down.

seventeen days. One was dead, and the other two were so weak that they could barely stand.[7] All of the bark within reach of the starving animals had been chewed off the cedars to which they were tied.

While Jim Shirley—the bandit leader—was a comparative stranger in Meeker, H. S. Harp, a cattleman of that area, claimed that Shirley had worked for him at one time. Harp referred to him as "one of the pleasantest fellows I ever met, a dandy stock tender, a good cook, and a man who always kept a clean cabin."[8]

As time went on, it was learned that the other two bandits—George Law and The Kid—were well known in the Browns Park country of northwestern Colorado, where Law had worked for the Lily Park Cattle Company.[9]  However, even in Browns Park no one knew the real name of The Kid other than the probably ficticious one of Pierce. It was believed that he was one of two men who held up the Meeker-Rifle stage about a year before.[10]  H. S. Harp, who was acquainted with Shirley, said that The Kid originally came to Colorado from Wyoming.[11]

The two warning shots, coupled with the additional five minutes taken to gather and break the rifles in the store, sealed the fate of the bungling bank robbers. But even if these two fatal mistakes had not been made, the robbery still would have failed. For, after the gunfire had died away, the sugar sack containing the loot was found in the bank office! The bandits, in their excitement, had forgotten it.

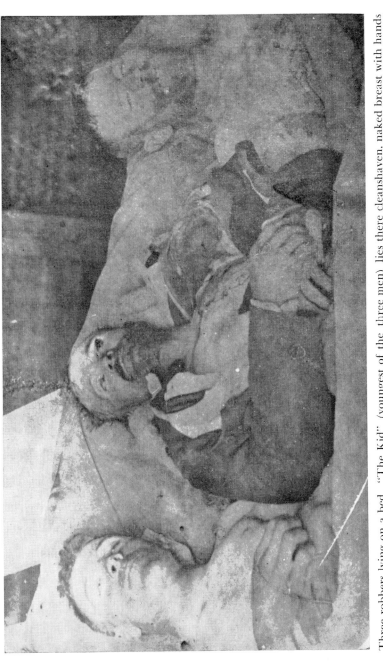

Three robbers lying on a bed. "The Kid" (youngest of the three men) lies there cleanshaven, naked breast with hands folded, nostrils up and eyes open; Jim Shirley lies in the middle with ruffled hair, heavy beard, dark moustache, clothes torn wide open on his breast, bullet wound in his left breast; George Law sleeps with his eyes closed, teeth gritted, heavy dark moustache, naked breasts with bullet wound in right breast.

92 SUNSET SLOPE

FOOTNOTES

[1]Interview with H. S. Harp, a witness to the robbery, Rio Blanco Co., C.W.A. Interviews for Colo. Hist. Society, 1933-34, pp. 187-188.

[2]*The Meeker Herald,* Oct. 17, 1896, article copied in Rio Blanco Co., C.W.A. Interviews, 1933-34, pp. 76-79. *The Meeker Herald* referred to the bandits as George Harris, Charles Jones, and Billy Smith, since at this time their real names were not known.

[3]*Souvenir History of J. W. Hugus & Co.,* published 1908, Rio Blanco Co., C.W.A. Interviews, 1933-34, pp. 40-47.

[4]*The Meeker Herald,* October 31, 1896. Article covering discovery of robbers' horses and camp copied in Rio Blanco Co., C.W.A. Interviews, p. 80. In possession of State Historical Society of Colorado.

[5]Rio Blanco Co., C.W.A. Interviews, 1933-34, p. 81. This article describes pictures of dead bank robbers taken where they lay.

[6]These were the names used in *The Meeker Herald* account on Oct. 17, 1896.

[7]*The Meeker Herald,* Oct. 31, 1896.

[8]Harp, *op. cit.,* p. 188.

[9]*The Meeker Herald,* Nov. 14, 1896. Article copied in Rio Blanco Co., C.W.A. Interviews, p. 80.

[10]*Ibid.*

[11]Harp, *op. cit.,* p. 188.

# VI

# FRIENDS FALL OUT

Residents of Grand Lake, county seat of Grand County,[1] started celebrating early on the morning of July 4, 1883. The clear, promising holiday was greeted with a thunderous welcome as early-risers fired their guns out over the big lake. Some of the better marksmen were spinning a ball across the water.

In somber contrast to this festivity, a small group of tense-faced, armed men walked up to the Fairview Hotel's small ice house. Tying bandanas over their faces, they hid themselves in the bushes on each side of the path which led to the county court house. One of the men was carrying a forty-foot rope, which he tossed beside a tall tree with a handy side-arm branch.[2]

Three members of this sinister looking party consisted of Grand County's most prominent citizens. One was J. G. Mills, chairman of the Board of County Commissioners.

Another was Charles Royer, sheriff of Grand County; and
the third was William Redman, undersheriff.

Within a few minutes after the men in ambush had
taken their positions, three other county officials stepped
out on the porch of the Fairview House and started up the
pathway toward the court house.[3] They were E. P. Weber,
a county commissioner; T. J. "Cap" Dean, the county
clerk; and Barney Day, the third county commissioner. As
they aproached the ice house, which stood about five hundred yards from the hotel, they little realized that they
were walking into a death trap, which was to climax nearly
a year of feuding between County Commissioners Mills
and Weber.

Mills and Weber both came to Colorado from Illinois,
where they had been good friends. Their friendship continued for some time after they established their homes in
the Grand Lake region. They had many interests in com-
mon. Each was successful in his particular field. Mills
became an outstanding lawyer of Teller City, largest mining town of the Grand Lake region at that time, and Weber
attained distinction as manager of the big Wolverine mine
at the rival mining town of Gaskill. Both men belonged
to the Republican party, and each took an active part in
local politics.

The breach started in 1882 at the Republican county
convention in Gaskill, which was held to elect two delegates to the state convention at Denver. Mills and Weber
were among the candidates, and in a heated contest Mills
and a man by the name of Charles Caswell were elected to
represent Grand County.

Refusing to admit defeat, Weber went to the state convention with his political standby, "Cap" Dean, as a contesting delegation. Delegates to the Denver convention voted to seat Weber and Dean over the rightfully elected Caswell and Mills.

When the quick-tempered Mills saw Weber that evening in front of the Brown Hotel, he stopped his old friend and threatened, "Some day we'll have this out in Grand County!"[4] From that time on they seldom spoke to each other.

After returning home, the misunderstanding widened as the two men opposed each other's policies at the county commissioner meetings. Other county officers became involved in the feud.

Undersheriff Bill Redman, who had trouble with Weber in 1880 over a mine, sided with Mills. Weber was vindictive toward anyone who crossed him, and the undersheriff received much sympathy throughout the county in his difficulties with the county commissioner.[5]

Sheriff Charles Royer defended his assistant against the quarrelsome Weber, and the sheriff thereby got mixed up in the controversy also on the side of Mills.

In addition to "Cap" Dean, the county clerk who helped unseat Mills at the state convention, Weber had the backing of Barney Day, the third county commissioner.

The feud finally came to a head on July 3, 1883. The county commissioners were supposed to hold their regular meeting on this day, but Mills, who had an important case in court, persuaded Weber and Day to postpone the meeting until July 5th.

In spite of this agreement, Weber and Day went ahead
and met secretly on the original date with County Clerk
"Cap" Dean also in attendance. In an effort to oust the
sheriff and undersheriff, the two commissioners voted to
raise the bonds of county officers to the impractical sum
of twenty or thirty thousand dollars.[6] Since there were no
bonding companies in those days, such a bond would be
impossible for the county officials to meet.

When the news of the secret commissioners' meeting
reached the hot-headed Mills that night, he was so indignant that he made arrangements with Sheriff Royer and
Undersheriff Redman to stage a mock lynching party and
scare Weber and his two cohorts out of the country.[7]

So, about nine o'clock the next morning Mills, the
sheriff, the deputy sheriff, along with several others who
came to watch the fun, hid themselves near the ice house of
the Fairview Hotel,[8] where the three victims were staying.

A short time later Weber, Dean, and Day came out of
the hotel and proceeded up the pathway toward the court
house. When they neared the prospective lynching tree,
Mills noticed that they were carrying guns, apparently
anticipating trouble.

As Mills watched Weber approach, he made up his
mind not to let this man make a fool of him again. He recalled how Weber had unseated him at the state convention nearly a year ago. Yesterday, his unscrupulous enemy
had once more double-crossed him and, taking advantage
of his absence, had, to all practical purposes, kicked Mills'
political allies out of their jobs. Now, apparently fore-
warned, Weber, who had thwarted Mills so many times in

the past, was on the verge of doing it again since the peaceful lynching party that Mills had planned was out of the question against men who were armed and prepared for trouble.

As Mills nursed his grievances, his hatred and frustration suddenly overruled his better judgment. He did the only thing that he could think of at the moment to even up the score. He jerked up his rifle and fired at his tormentor. Weber dropped in his tracks, critically wounded.

This started the shooting. Following his leader's example, Undersheriff Redman shot "Cap" Dean through the forehead, but the bleeding county clerk mustered sufficient strength to back-track toward the Fairview House. Before he had gone far, Mills jumped out from behind the bushes and overtook him. He knocked Dean down, and started to beat him over the head with his gun.

Commissioner Day, who had ducked in back of the ice house when the firing commenced, saw the masked man beating Dean. Stepping out from behind the small building, he shot Mills, who crumpled up in the pathway.

Again seeking shelter behind the ice house, Day met Redman. Firing from the hip, Day broke the undersheriff's right arm, and Redman's rifle dropped to the ground.

Before he could fire again, Sheriff Royer, seeing his assistant's danger, arose from his hiding place and shot Day, who fell backward into the lake.

The violent outbreak of shots was plainly heard over the morning's general commotion. However, most of the townspeople believed it to be just a part of the celebration. Several roomers at the Fairview House, who had seen the county clerk and the two commissioners disappear in the general direction of the reports, were not so sure, and they hastened to the scene of the tragedy.

Mills, still wearing his mask, was found dead in the trail. Day, who had been shot through the heart, lay part way in the lake. "Cap" Dean was sprawled on his stomach, bleeding at the forehead. At first glance he looked as if he were dead, but he was still breathing. Weber, who was also alive, lay unconscious by the ice house in a pool of blood.

Weber and Dean were carried back to the Fairview House. Weber died that night. In his pockets were found several copies of the fateful resolution passed by him and Day in secret session to raise the bond of county officials.

"Cap" Dean, the county clerk, was up and around several days later, but about two weeks later he died unexpectedly in an upstairs bedrom of the Fairview House.

Mrs. Mary Young, owner of the hotel, never succeeded in entirely obliterating the blood stains on her floor, where the two wounded men had been carried in. The sawdust around her ice house was also discolored with the crimson stains for a long time afterwards.

After the gun fight Sheriff Royer set spur to his horse and galloped all the way to Hot Sulphur Springs. He visited with several people there but never mentioned the Grand Lake trouble. He changed mounts and continued on to Georgetown, where he stayed at the Ennis Hotel. Several months later the landlady of the hotel found him dead in his room with a bullet hole in his head. His revolver lay beside him, and it was generally believed that the conscience-stricken sheriff had committed suicide.

Grand Lake as it looked at time of the killings. *Photo courtesy of Denver Public Library Western Collection. Photo by George Dalgleish.*

However, the landlady and her family always suspected that the sheriff had been murdered due to the strange position of his six-shooter relative to the bullet wound.[9] As further evidence of foul-play, Royer was in possession of a large sum of money the night before his death, and this money was gone when the body was discovered.[10]

A few months after Royer's death, Frank S. Byers, widely known pioneer of Hot Sulphur Springs, reported that Sheriff Royer had made a full confession and statement concerning the facts of the Grand Lake killings to Adam King, owner of a ranch below Hot Sulphur Springs. Royer was alleged to have concluded his confession by saying:

> "Ever since I killed him (Barney Day) . . . old Barney has been looking me in the eye. Ad, I can't stand it any longer. I can't make a move that I am not watched, and it is only a question of time before it will come to a show-down. I have decided to make short work of the whole mess."[11]

Even more mysterious was the fate of Undersheriff Redman, sixth victim of the Grand Lake feud. On August 7th, a month after the violent battle, several Utah cowboys ran across a dead man lying in the trail about fifteen miles from the Ouray Ute Indian Agency. He had not been dead long—probably about two days. He was lying on his back in his blankets. A bullet hole through the temple was apparently the cause of death. A six-shooter with one empty cartridge was found between his knees. It looked a little like suicide except that there were no powder marks on the man's upturned face. Closer investigation revealed fifty dollars sewed up in his shirt. A rid-ing saddle and pack saddle had been thrown beside the trail, and two horses grazed a short distance away.[12]

One of the cowboys rode to the agency to report the discovery, while the others continued on with the herd. The next morning Major J. F. Minniss, the agent, and half a dozen Ute Indians accompanied the cowboy back to the body. As they were looking about for clues, one of the Indians called the agent's attention to the name "William Redman" traced nearby in the ground. Soon afterward the agent found the same name scratched upon the dead man's saddle, "William Redman, Middle Park, Colorado."

The corpse had such extraordinarily large feet and hands that they were noticed immediately. This was one of Undersheriff Redman's outstanding characteristics. Ap-parently the dead man was Redman, who had been killed by his Grand County enemies while he slept. The presence of the six-shooter with the empty chamber could have been a clumsy effort on their part to make the deputy's death look like suicide.

For a while these conclusions satisfied everyone as to Redman's fate. But, as man after man began insisting that they had seen Redman in any number of places, including Arizona, Wyoming and Missouri, people began to doubt that the murdered man in Utah was Redman after all.

Other versions of what happened to the undersheriff began to replace the old one. Bob Wheeler claimed that Redman escaped to Arizona after the Grand Lake killing and became the leader of a band of outlaws known as the Redman Gang.[13] Bass Redman, brother of the mystery man, told Judge Jacob Pettingell that after brooding about the Grand Lake killing for months, the undersheriff finally shot himself back of his cabin near Encampment, Wyoming.[14] But Bass might have said this to protect his brother from the law and avenging enemies. So, Redman's actual fate still remains as much a mystery as ever.

The morning of July 4, 1883, had all the promise of a happy holiday, but it proved to be the most tragic day in all of Grand Lake's history.

FOOTNOTES

[1]Grand Lake was the county seat of Grand County from 1881 to 1888.

[2]Charles H. Leckenby, *The Tread of Pioneers,* Steamboat Pilot, 1945, p. 109.

[3]Mary Lyons Cairns, *The Pioneers,* World Press, Inc., Denver, Colo., 1946, p. 223.

[4]Leckenby, *op. cit.,* pp. 107-108.

[5]*The Prospector,* July 12, 1883.

[6]Leckenby, *op. cit.,* pp. 108-109.

[7]Cairns, *op. cit.,* p. 228 (alleged statement of Sheriff Charles Royer).

[8]*Ibid.*

[9]Leckenby, *op. cit.,* p. 110.

[10]*Ibid.*

[11]Cairns, *op. cit.,* p. 228.

[12]*Op. cit.,* pp. 235-236.

[13]*Ibid.*

[14]Leckenby, *op. cit.,* p. 110.

*VII*

# THE MANEATER

Twenty-one exhausted prospectors trudged up the Uncompahgre River toward Chief Ouray's winter camp on the Ute Indian reservation near the present site of Montrose, Colorado. It was just past the middle of November, 1873, and the surrounding mountains were covered with snow. The prospectors had traveled more than 300 miles from Salt Lake City to get an early entry into the newly discovered gold and silver fields of southwestern Colorado.[1] The party had encountered trackless wastes, deep snows, and wide rivers. They had built a raft to ford the Green River, but upon reaching the rapid midstream current the raft went out of control and most of their provisions and equipment went overboard.[2]

Salvaging what they could, the gold seekers continued their tramp toward the Grand River,[3] averaging about ten miles a day. Nine days later they forded the Grand near

the present city of Grand Junction and camped on the
south side of the river. While encamped there on the Ute
reservation, three Indians rode up. They informed the
hard-pressed explorers that Chief Ouray's camp was only
"three sleeps away" and instructed them how to reach it.[4]

When the heavily bearded, half-starved men stumbled
into Ouray's winter camp three days later, the famous
chief and his wife Chipeta hospitably received the tres-
passers on the Ute reservation. Ouray told them that it
would be foolhardy to try crossing the high mountain
ranges so late in the season and invited the white men to
spend the winter with him.

For three weeks the prospectors remained with the Indians, regaining their strength after all the hardships that
they had endured.

One evening as the twenty-one men sat about a big
fire eating supper O. D. Loutsenhizer said, "It won't take
much longer for a party this size to eat our host out of
house and home. I don't know about the rest of you, but
I'm ready to hit the trail for Saguache."[5]

"I'll go along with you, Lot," a high squeaky voice answered. "I know a short cut that'll make the trip a hell of
a lot shorter."

The speaker was a tall, gaunt, broad-shouldered young
man of about twenty-four. A matted black beard partially
covered a wax-like complexion, and his large but abruptly
sloping head gave him the peculiar appearance of having
no forehead.[6]

"You don't know this country any better than I do,

Packer," Lot said sarcastically. "We should have left you in jail."

Packer looked threateningly at Lot and muttered some obscenity under his breath. Alfred Packer was not popular with the group. When the expedition was being organized, he was in the Salt Lake City jail for passing counterfeit money.[7] The landlord of a miners' boarding house, where the prospectors had assembled prior to their departure, told them that Packer was familiar with the Colorado Territory and might prove to be a valuable guide if they would get him released from jail by paying his fine. The fine was paid, and Packer became the twenty-first member of the group.[8] However, events proved that while Packer may have been in Colorado, he was not acquainted with the region where the gold seekers were bound. He was not only a poor guide, but also his illiteracy, sullen taciturnity, and apparent dullness made him an undesirable companion.

The next morning, against the advice of their host, Lot and four companions started out for the small trading post of Saguache some one hundred miles away. Ouray told them how to get to their destination by way of the agency cow-camp and the Los Pinos agency. Just before they left, he warned them never to lose sight of the Gunnison and to attempt no short cuts.

Five days later Packer persuaded five others to attempt the trip. The remaining ten Utah men settled down until spring. Within three days after the Packer group left Ouray's camp, they were in serious trouble. Their small supply of food was exhausted, and they had used all of

their matches. Carrying a life-saving fire in an old coffee
pot, they fought their way through the deep snow. At
night and the early mornings the temperature ranged from
forty to fifty degrees below zero.

Game was scarce in the high mountains at this time
of year, but the desperate men staved off starvation by a
meager diet of berries, roots, buds and bark. Occasionally
they shot a rabbit or squirrel. They were even forced to
boil their moccasins and eat them.[9]

When about twelve miles from the agency's cow-camp,
Packer, disregarding Ouray's advice, turned southward
from the Gunnison in an attempt to take a short cut to
the agency.

By the time they reached Lake San Cristobal about two
and a half miles southeast of the present site of Lake City,
the exhausted men realized that they could not keep going
much longer. They built a fire and established their camp
between a steep overhanging cliff and a grove of spruce
trees.[10]

"I'm clean gone," Israel Swan, the oldest man of the
group said. "Packer, why don't you walk up to the top of
the hill over there and see if you can locate the agency?"[11]

"That's a good idea," Shannon Bell agreed. "We'll
have a good fire ready for you when you get back."

Using his rifle as a walking stick, Packer struggled slowly up the mountain through the deep snow. On his way
he found some rose berries and buds which he ate.[12] The
mountain summit furnished a splendid view of the surrounding country, but there was no sign of human life.
Disheartened, Packer retraced his steps.

It was getting dark when he joined the others around the fire.[13]

"Any luck?" George Noon asked expectantly.

Packer shook his head despondently.

"I don't believe you know where you're at, Packer," Bell said. "We should never have taken that short cut."

"The agency is farther away than I thought," Packer said, "but I know the general location."

"Like hell you do," Frank Miller snapped, his nerves on edge. "We're lost, and you might as well admit it."

That night as the six men lay side by side in their blankets, Packer, half-crazed from hunger, weariness and exposure, brooded about what his companions had said. As he nursed his imaginary grievances and considered his desperate plight, a diabolical plan took shape in his confused, agitated mind.

About midnight Packer raised up to look at the five men stretched out on the ground beside him. All appeared to be sound asleep. Quietly crawling out of his blankets, Packer walked silently over to the campfire and grabbed a hatchet. Then, with an insane gleam in his eye, he slowly and stealthily approached the sleepers. . . .

One evening two months later in March, Alonzo Hartman was gathering some wood at the Los Pinos agency, located about twenty-five miles south of the present site of Gunnison. Winters are always severe at the agency and only a few employees had remained. With the exception of Hartman, they were sitting around a stove in the bunkhouse reading or playing cards.

As Hartman loaded the wood on his arm he saw a man walking toward the agency. He was carrying a gun and a little pack strapped around his shoulders. Hartman blinked his eyes in amazement since the nearest habitation was fifty miles away.[14]

"Hello," Hartman greeted when the man walked up, "are you lost?"

"Is this the agency?" the stranger asked. His hair and beard were long and matted, but he showed few signs of having suffered from exposure and hunger.

Hartman told him that it was and took him to the agent's office, where Stephen A. Dole was in charge during the absence of General Charles Adams.

The newcomer introduced himself as Alfred Packer and asked for a drink of whiskey.[15]

After Packer was fed and clothed, he told his story. He said that he and five companions had started out from Ouray's winter camp on the Uncompahgre with the intention of stopping at the government cow-camp on the Gunnison.[16] After traveling for a few days he hurt his leg and was unable to walk. The others, not wishing to waste precious time waiting for him to recuperate and disagreeing with him as to which way they should go, deserted him and started southward in the direction of Silverton. After a few days' rest, he was able to resume his journey, and with great difficulty had finally found his way to the agency, subsisting on berries and an occasional rabbit or squirrel which he had managed to kill. He told Stephen A. Dole that his five comrades had by this time undoubtedly reached Silverton or the Animas Valley.

Alfred Packer—the maneater—as he looked in Gunnison at the time of second trial. *Photo courtesy of Denver Public Library Western Collection.*

The listeners expressed sympathy for all the hardships that he had undergone, and Dole offered him a job in order to help him make a few dollars before he continued on his way. Packer refused the job, but sold his rifle to one of the employees for ten dollars. He then left for Saguache forty-five miles away, saying that he had all he wanted of Colorado and desired to return to his family and friends in Pennsylvania.

A few days after he left the agency some Indians discovered and brought in strips of flesh, which the agency doctor identified as having been cut from a human body. Since they were found on Packer's trail, Acting Agent Dole assumed that Packer had killed the members of his party and lived off their flesh.[17]

At Saguache Packer stayed for six days with Larry Dolan, an Irish saloon keeper. Dolan was surprised at the comparatively large sums of money that the newcomer occasionally displayed. Packer spent most of his time at Saguache in drinking, carousing and playing poker.

Soon after his arrival Packer met various members of the original party of twenty-one prospectors. Lot's group, who had left Ouray's camp before Packer, had twice nearly perished in the mountains. Those who had waited until spring made the journey without mishap. They inquired about Packer's five companions, and he told them that they were probably in Silverton since they started out in that direction when they left him after he became lame.

During his stay Packer went to Mears' store and bought a horse for seventy dollars. He paid the money in bank notes, but Otto Mears, having been told of Packer's jail sentence for passing counterfeit money, refused to accept one of the bills which looked to him like a counterfeit. Packer thereupon pulled out another pocketbook and took from it another bill, which Mears accepted.[18] Upon seeing the two pocketbooks Mears immediately suspected that Packer had murdered and robbed his companions in the mountains.

Members of the Utah party began to suspect the same thing when they noticed that Packer had much more than the original twenty dollars with which he had started out from Salt Lake. Once, in a state of intoxication, he had exhibited a pipe, a pocket-knife, and some other small articles which were known to have belonged to the missing men.

Six days after Packer reached Saguache, General Adams, the Los Pinos agent, stopped there enroute back to the agency from Denver. Mears told him about the strangeness of Packer's arrival at the agency and how he had two pocketbooks, both containing money. Several of the Utah men also related their suspicions to the Indian agent.

Adams decided that if he could induce Packer to return to the agency with him where he had full jurisdiction, he could either force a confession or hold him prisoner until an investigation could be made.

By this time it became known that none of Packer's companions had reached Silverton or the Animas Valley, which convinced Adams that they had either been killed by Packer or had perished in the deep snow.

Adams told Packer that if he would act as a guide a party would be outfitted at the agency to look for the missing men. After much reluctance and numerous excuses, Packer finally consented to do so if Adams would bear all the expenses. So, Packer was brought back to the agency, accompanied by Mears and several of the Utah men.

In crossing Cochetopa Creek Packer threw something into the water. When asked what it was, he said that it was some trash that he wanted to get rid of. Upon reaching the agency at dark, Adams asked Packer to come to his office.

"Mr. Mears informs me that you had two pocketbooks at Saguache. I want to see them."

"I don't have no pocketbooks," Packer answered sullenly.

"Search him, Otto," Adams said to Mears. However, nothing but a long-bladed knife was found.

"Those pocketbooks must have been what you threw into the creek this afternoon," Adams continued.

Packer remained silent, his dull mind responding with its usual slowness.

"Where did you get the large sums of money shown at Saguache? You only had ten dollars from the sale of your gun when you left here."[19]

"I borrowed the money from a friend."

"What was his name?"

Packer hesitated. "I can't remember."

"Listen here, Packer," Adams said impatiently. "You can't think fast enough to lie and get away with it. It is perfectly obvious that everything you have told me so far is false. It all points to the fact that you are afraid to tell the truth because you murdered your comrades. Now, I want to know and will know what became of your companions that you left in the mountains."

Packer, now thoroughly alarmed, told Adams that his five companions had died from hunger and exposure at various stages of the journey and that since burial was impossible their bodies were left as they had died.

General Adams stood up and walked over to the confused man. "Packer," he said, "you are still lying. Shortly after you left the agency some Indians brought in strips of meat which they found along your trail. The agency physician said that those strips of flesh were cut from a human body."

Confronted with this evidence, Packer admitted that he had subsisted on the flesh of his companions. He then told a fantastic story of how Israel Swan, the oldest man of the party, had died from starvation and that the remaining five in their starving condition had eaten some of the flesh of the dead man.[20] He went on to say that as the plight of the survivors became more and more desperate they had drawn lots to decide who should be killed next to supply food for those who were left. By this process, Shanon Bell and Packer finally became the sole survivors. They agreed not to harm each other, but after living for several days on roots, Bell attacked Packer. Packer was then forced to kill Bell in self-defense. He cut up the body and ate as much as he could. Then he packed away some for future use. When he reached the Los Pinos agency, he threw away the human flesh that he was carrying.[21]

General Adams did not believe this weird story, but

he outfitted a search party to find Bell's body and asked Packer to go along as guide.[22] The search party consisted of several of the Utah prospectors, two agency employees and three or four Indians, all under the charge of Herman F. Lauter, clerk of the agency. On the fourth day out Packer portrayed his natural viciousness by trying to stab the clerk when Lauter accused him of being a cannibal.[23]

After a two weeks' search, Packer claimed that he was lost.

Preston Nutter, one of the original Utah party, exclaimed, "You ain't lost, Packer! I'm satisfied that you killed those men and ought to be hanged for it."

"If that's the way you feel," Packer flared back, "you find them!"

The search party returned to the agency, and General Adams had Packer arrested. He was taken to Saguache and turned over to the sheriff of that county to be held for trial. Within a short time he escaped and was not heard of again for nearly ten years.

A few months later in June of 1874, most of the deep snow had disappeared in the mountains, and prospectors began to pass by the agency in their search for gold. General Adams told them to look for the bodies of the five missing men.

One of the first to go to the Lake San Cristobal area that summer was J. A. Randolph, a photographer who sketched scenery and took pictures for *Harper's Weekly*. When about two and one-half miles southeast of the present site of Lake City, he discovered Packer's grisly secret.

The decomposed, mutilated bodies of Packer's five

This picture of the maneater's victims appeared in *Harper's Weekly* October 17, 1874. Photo courtesy of Denver Public Library Western Collection.

companions lay between an overhanging cliff and a clump of spruce. Four of them lay in a row within arm's length of each other while the fifth, who was identified as Shannon Bell, lay some distance from the others. The skulls of all the victims had been split open with a hatchet, and Shannon Bell had in addition been shot through the back.

Preston Nutter came from Saguache to identify the bodies, which were buried on the eastern shore of Lake San Cristobal just where they were discovered. The burial ground is now surrounded by an iron enclosure, and a bronze tablet on a huge natural rock reads:

> This Tablet erected in memory of Israel Swan, George Noon, Frank Miller, James Humphries, and Shannon Bell who were murdered on this spot early in the year 1874 while pioneering the mineral resources of the San Juan country.

Apparently Packer killed all the men with a hatchet while they slept. Bell, the last man to be murdered, probably awakened and started to run. Packer shot him in the back and then hit him on the head with his hatchet.

Contrary to his first confession to General Adams, the victims had all died together. So, it was obvious why Packer wasn't anxious to find the bodies when he was a guide for the search party.

A hastily built cabin was found near the corpses,[24] where Packer had lived for nearly two months, subsisting on the frozen flesh of the dead men. In the last of his numerous and contradictory confessions told at the Lake City trial,[25] Packer related how for a period of about two

months he cut off the flesh and cooked it. In March, when
the weather grew warmer, he filled a cartridge sack with
this food supply and, carrying the coffee pot with a fire in
it, started out in search of the agency. He admitted taking
with him the money and personal articles of his dead comrades. When he camped three-quarters of a mile from the
agency, he had three pieces of meat and some rose buds.
The next day when he saw the agency he threw away the
fire and the flesh and carried in only his sack and gun.[26]

In March, 1883, nearly ten years after Packer's escape,
Jean Cazauhon, one of the original Utah group, heard
voices of men through a thin partition of a house at Fort
Fetterman, Wyoming Territory. The Frenchman instantly
recognized Packer's peculiar, high-pitched voice, and, in-
quiring about the man, learned that Packer was residing
there under the assumed name of John Schwartze.[27]

Cazauhon sent word of the fugitive's whereabouts to
General Adams, who was then holding the position of
United States Post Office Inspector. Adams communicated
with the sheriff of that area, who arrested Packer and held
him until Adams arrived. Adams took him to Denver and
put him in jail. From there he was taken to Lake City,
the county seat of Hinsdale County, by the Hinsdale County sheriff to stand trial at the opening term of the district
court. There, on April 14, 1883, Melville B. Gerry, the
District Judge, sentenced Packer to be hanged on May 19,
1883, at a place to be prepared in Lake City for this purpose.

Judge Gerry who pronounced sentence was a recent
arrival from Georgia and an ardent Democrat. Lake City

and Hinsdale County were strongly Republican. Larry Dolan, Packer's roommate during his six-day sojourn at Saguache, had moved to Lake City and opened a saloon after the discovery of gold in that area. He was quite a wit and took advantage of the Judge's politics to give his version of the sentence.

"The Judge, he says, 'Stand up, you man-eatin' son of a bitch, stand up!' Then, pointin' his finger at him so ragin' mad he was, he says, 'They was seven Democrats in Hinsdale County and you ate five of them, God damn you. I sentence you to be hanged by the neck until you are dead, dead, dead, as a warning against reducin' the Democratic population of the State.' "[28]

Dolan's account of the sentence has become almost as well-known as the crime itself, and many people mistakenly believe that this was the language and manner used by Judge Gerry in sentencing Packer.

A gallows was erected near the spot where Packer had murdered his five victims. However, before his execution, the State Supreme Court ruled that a person could not be hanged in Colorado for committing a crime before Colorado became a state.[29] The Supreme Court ordered a new trial at Gunnison, where the people were not so prejudiced against Packer as they were at Lake City.

Packer was tried twice in Gunnison and was finally found guilty of voluntary manslaughter and sentenced on August 5, 1886, to forty years in the state penitentiary. He was thirty-four years old at the time.

After serving fifteen of his forty years, he was paroled by Governor Charles Thomas in January, 1901, after tremendous pressure was brought to bear by the *Denver Post* to free Packer. The chief argument given for the parole was that his cannibalism was done under the pressure of starvation, which caused him not to be fully responsible for his actions at the time.[30] Packer was not allowed to leave the state or correspond further with his relatives in Pennsylvania, whom he was continually threatening to kill.[31]

Ten years after he was paroled, Colorado's maneater died in January, 1911, at Littleton. He was fifty-nine years old. For some unknown reason he was buried in the Civil War Veteran's Cemetery of that city although so far as anyone knows he never fought in the Civil War.[32]

So, from beginning to end, the Packer case is probably one of the greatest travesties of justice in the history of the state.

FOOTNOTES

[1]William C. Blair, "The Story of Packer, the Maneater," *Silver World,* Dec. 4, 1930.

[2]Sidney Jocknick, *Early Days on the Western Slope of Colorado,* The Carson-Harper Co., Denver, Colo., 1913, pp. 62-63.

[3]Now called the Colorado.

[4]Jocknick, *op. cit.,* pp. 62-63.

[5]*Ibid.,* p. 59.

[6]Arthur W. Monroe, *San Juan Silver,* privately pub. 1940, p. 13. So described by Charles F. Huntsman of Montrose who was going to school in Lake City at the time of Packer's first trial.

[7]Jocknick, *op. cit.,* p. 72.

[8]*Ibid.,* p. 61.

[9]Blair, *op. cit.*

[10]Edward V. Dunklee, "Colorado Cannibalism," *Brand Book,* Denver, Colorado, 1947.

[11]Blair, *op. cit.,* Packer's story told at the Lake City trial of the last day the six camped alive together.

[12]*Ibid.*

[13]According to Packer's story at his Lake City trial, Shannon Bell had killed the men during Packer's absence and attacked him upon his return. This part of the story was in all probability false, and I am reconstructing the events of that tragic evening in accordance with the preponderance of evidence.

[14]Alonzo Hartman, "Memories and Experiences with the Utes in Colorado," original manuscript, copied in master's thesis of John B. Lloyd, entitled "The Uncompahgre Utes," Western State College, Mar. 24, 1939. In possession of History Dept. of Denver Public Library, pp. 5-15.

[15]Jocknick, *op. cit.,* p. 71.

[16]*Ibid.,* p. 70.

[17]*Ibid.,* p. 72.

[18]*Ibid.*

[19]*Ibid.,* p. 75.

[20]Blair, *op. cit.*

[21]Dunklee, *op. cit.*

[22]*Ibid.*

[23]Jocknick, *op. cit.,* p. 76.

[24]*Ibid.,* p. 78.

[25]". . . That same night I took blankets and covered them (the bodies) up. I sat there all night. The next morning the bodies were froze. I took the kettle and started away but had to go back. I went into the pine, built a fire and cooked some of the flesh. Right there was my last feeling. I eat that meat. That's what hurts me and has for the last nine years. I can't tell how long I was there. I was perfectly happy and contented. I did not suffer and did not think of the agency. I just wanted to sleep. But after a while fear came back to me. I seemed to think of the agency. I started twice with fire in a coffee pot and

no provisions and twice had to come back. In March the snow began to have a crust. I went back to the bodies, cut off some flesh with the butcher knife and cooked it and filled a cartridge sack to carry with me. When I went to cut the flesh with Miller's knife I found a pocketbook with $70. I took the money. Perhaps it was wrong but I took it. I had $20 of my own. . . . I don't know how many days I traveled. . . ."

[26]Blair, *op. cit.*

[27]Jocknick, *op. cit.*, p. 78.

[28]Blair, *op. cit.*

[29]It became a state in 1876.

[30]Charles S. Thomas, a letter written by Thomas to William C. Blair, *The Silver World*, Dec. 4, 1930.

[31]*Ibid.*

[32]Dunklee, *op. cit.*

Ben Lowe's Last Picture. This picture was taken just two days before fatal gun duel in Escalante Canyon. It shows rugged Ben Lowe with his two sons, Robert and William, near their home in Escalante Canyon. *Photo courtesy of John*

# *VIII*

# THE ESCALANTE CANYON DUEL

Early one summer afternoon Ben Lowe and his two young sons walked their horses slowly down the winding Escalante Canyon road toward home. The boys, attired in chaps, slouchy sombreros, and spurred boots, looked like miniature editions of the big cattleman who rode beside them.

From time to time Ben's hot-blooded horse snorted and shied at various objects along the way, but the veteran cowboy gauged the unexpected jolts with flawless timing, and scarcely moved in the saddle.

Suddenly he glanced back over his shoulder to see another rider rapidly approaching around a bend in the road. His face grew tense as he looked back again and again to observe that the rider was soon going to overtake them.

"Boys," he said finally, pulling his lively mount to a stop, "ride on ahead. Here comes Cash, and I want to talk with him alone."

As the boys trotted along to keep their lead, they could hear their father and Cash talking loudly and angrily. Then, unexpectedly the conversation was terminated by three gunshots, which echoed and re-echoed through the canyon.

Startled, the boys galloped back around the bend to see what had happened. There they discovered the tragic end to a dramatic story which started many years before:

Two prominent cattlemen of Delta County at the turn of the century were Ben Lowe and Cassius Sampson, and both ran their cattle on the Escalante Canyon range midway between Delta and Grand Junction.

They were very different types of people. Ben Lowe had a reckless sweep about him which aroused the admiration of less colorful men. He liked to ride spirited horses and presented an imposing figure in the saddle. He was a crack shot with any kind of gun and was a familiar figure at Delta County rodeos where he won many a calf-roping contest with his accurate lasso. He was notably generous and loyal to his friends, but toward his enemies, bitter and uncompromising.[1]

Cash Sampson, on the other hand, was a small, quiet man. But what he lacked in size and color, he made up for in nerve, and he was probably the most celebrated peace officer that Delta County ever had. For, in addition to his cattle interests, Cash, at various times in his career, held the man-sized jobs of sheriff, brand inspector, and deputy United States marshal.[2]

In these capacities he ran counter to Ben Lowe, who was a leader of the cattlemen who were trying to keep sheep out of the country around Delta. At that time sheep were not grazed scientifically, and Delta cattlemen, who had occupied this range first, feared that the woolly hordes, if allowed to enter, would grub down and trample out the grass on this unregulated territory.

While Cash Sampson's sympathies were with the cattlemen, as an officer of the law, it was his duty to oppose the forceful measures occasionally taken by his hard-riding, quick-triggered friends. Sheep had been run over high bluffs, sheepherders shot at, and some of their mules killed by unidentified cowboys, who became known as the Night Riders.

Troublemakers told Ben Lowe that Cash had taken sides with the sheepmen and was out to arrest him as a ringleader of the cattle interests.

The same gossips also informed Cash that Ben was talking loud behind the lawman's back, calling him a sheeplover and turncoat.

As the misunderstanding between the two former friends continued to grow, their dislike for each other became legendary, and many Delta County residents prophesied that sooner or later they would have it out.

That day finally came on June 9, 1917.[3] About tenthirty on that fateful morning Cash rode down the Escalante Canyon road past Kelso Musser's cow-camp. He was on his way to Flat Mesa to look for strays. As customary in this western cattle country, Musser asked the passing rider to stay for dinner. Cash accepted and helped prepare the meal.

An hour later Ben Lowe and his two young sons,

Robert, aged eleven, and William, nine, rode by the Musser cow-camp. Under the circumstances, Musser might
have wished for different guests, but they were likewise invited to dinner.

At the table were Kelso Musser, Cash Sampson, Ben
Lowe and his sons, and a cowhand, "Shorty" Gibson.
While the two enemies did not direct any remarks toward
each other, they participated in the general conversation
and did not outwardly show any evidence of hostility. One
might have suspected that the talking progressed too
smoothly, that Cash and Ben were a shade too polite.

Both men were armed. Cash carried a revolver on his
hip, while Ben's six-shooter was in a shoulder holster under
his jumper.

After dinner Ben and his sons were the first to leave.
They mounted their horses and started down the canyon
road toward home.

Fifteen minutes later, right on two o'clock, Cash also
departed in the same direction, intending to turn off the
canyon road onto the Flat Mesa trail about two miles below the Musser cabin.

Cash's mount traveled at a running walk and made
better time than the Lowe horses. When Cash disappeared
among the cedars a half-mile below Musser's cabin, Shorty
Gibson remarked, "It looks like Cash'll overtake Ben before he reaches the turnoff trail."

"I hope he don't," Musser replied. "Talkin' won't
mend things."

When Ben saw Cash approaching, he told his boys to
ride on ahead. Robert and William trotted forward and

maintained a 75 to 100-yard lead. They could hear their father and Cash quarreling but could not see them because of the turns in the road.

No one will ever know the momentous subject about which the two men were arguing. However, it so happened that within the near future Cash was scheduled to testify against Ben before a grand jury that was investigating a case in which the Night Riders had stampeded some sheep and shot a sheepherder's mules. Cash tried to avoid testifying against a fellow-cattleman, but Ben did not know this, believing that his enemy was going to make a personal issue out of the matter. Consequently, it is quite possible that this pending grand jury investigation was the delicate topic of their heated conversation.

The discussion was suddenly interrupted by three shots fired in rapid succession.

As Robert and William turned back, they heard their father call to them.

They galloped around the bend to find Cash lying on his left side, dead, still clutching his revolver. His even-dispositioned horse was standing near-by.

About fifty feet away Ben was leaning dazedly against the trunk of a cedar, and the boys saw him take one more shot at Cash before slumping to the ground in a sitting position. He could not speak when Robert and William reached him and soon died, his six-shooter falling by his side. His spirited horse was not in sight, but the tracks showed that he had been reined abruptly to the right, apparently when Ben grabbed for his gun in its shoulder holster. Ordinarily Ben wore a belt holster, but it was being repaired at the time.

Robert sent William back to Kelso Musser's cabin while the older boy stayed by his father's body. William returned to the camp crying and greatly excited.

"Dad and Cash have killed each other down the road about a mile and a half," he told Musser and Gibson.

Musser saddled his horse and rode to Arthur Ward's ranch, a quarter of a mile away, to get his help in caring for the bodies. Ward caught a horse, and William took the men to the scene of the gun fight.

Upon examining the guns, they found that three chambers were empty in Ben Lowe's .45 caliber revolver. One of the bullets had struck Cash above his left ear and come out at the back, top portion of his head. Another slug had piercerd his left groin, and a third had missed its mark.

Only one chamber in Cash's .32-.20 caliber six-shooter was empty. This bullet had entered Ben's left side near the small of his back, passing upward through the lungs and coming out at his left breast. Ben had obviously been leaning forward in his saddle at the time he was shot. He bled to death within a few minutes.

No one was ever able to reconstruct the order of the duel, though gossips had their endless versions. Only the empty gun chambers, the bullet wounds, the position of the bodies, and the abrupt turning to the right of the tracks of Ben's horse remained to tell the tragic story.

Arthur Ward and Kelso Musser lifted the bodies into a wagon side by side and hauled them to Delta, arriving

Cash Sampson—who fell before the gunfire of Ben Lowe in Escalante Canyon duel, is shown here with pet dog. *Photo courtesy of Mrs. Dick Rober.*

there at about eleven o'clock that night. Shorty Gibson had preceded them and reported the calamitous news.

Cash was forty-six years old and unmarried. Ben was forty-nine and left a widow and five children—three daughters and the two sons.

It had been a long summer's day at a fair time of year. Not the kind of day for dying.

FOOTNOTES

[1]Interview with Mack Davis, sheriff of Delta County at time of gunfight, 1938.

[2]Interview with Mrs. Dick Raber, neice of Cash Sampson, 1952.

[3]*Delta County Tribune,* June 15, 1917, p. 1.

# IX

# THE MANHUNT

Sheriff Charles W. Neiman and Undersheriff Ethan Allen Farnham of Routt County walked their horses slowly across the ice-covered Little Snake River.[1] They were on their way to Brown's Park in the northwest corner of Colorado to arrest P. L. Johnson and Judge[2] Bennett, who had been accused of killing cattle on the range and selling the meat to operators of a copper mine and smelter on Douglas Mountain.

It was February 28, 1898, and at this time Brown's Park was a notorious hideout for outlaws. The park was a sparsely settled, cedar-covered basin surrounded by mountains. It was traversed from the northwest to the southeast by the Green River and overlapped into northeastern Utah and southwestern Wyoming.[3]

As the two officers jogged along, they became interested in the tracks of several horses which had recently entered the snow-crusted wagon road and were evidently traveling at a slow pace ahead of them.

Finally, upon rounding a bend they saw in the distance three horsemen, one of whom was leading a pack horse. As if not wanting to be overtaken, the riders suddenly turned off the road and headed for Douglas Mountain,[4] which stands in the right angle formed by the junction of the Green and Yampa rivers.

"I've got a hunch that two of those men are Johnson and Bennett," Undersheriff Farnham remarked. "Shall we follow 'em?"

"They'll be makin' camp for the night before long," Sheriff Neiman answered, "and we can pick up their trail the first thing in the mornin'."

It was dark when the officers reached Eb Bassett's ranch, where they intended to spend the night. Eb, a pioneer of the region, and a young man by the name of Strang greeted them as they rode up.

During supper Strang told the newcomers that Johnson —one of the men that the officers were after for cattle rustling—had killed his brother, William Strang, less than two weeks ago. He said that in a spirit of fun young William had pulled a chair back just as Johnson was sitting down in it for dinner at a cattle ranch just over the Wyoming line. Johnson whipped out his six-shooter and shot the boy, who died the next day.[5] A posse of Wyoming men had been looking for Johnson in Brown's Park but lost trace of him.

After supper Neiman called Strang aside and said, "Johnson may have been one of the men we saw this afternoon ridin' toward Douglas Mountain. Saddle a horse and get a posse here before mornin'. We'll pick up the trail at daybreak."

Shortly after midnight Strang returned with six horsemen, and as soon as it was daylight the man-hunters started out. They located the suspicious horse tracks and followed them all day. They finally led to the travelers' camp at the foot of Douglas Mountain. Apparently caught by surprise, the fugitives had left suddenly, leaving their horses, food, bedding, and camp utensils. Their footprints led up the mountain, which was covered with caves and rocks. Behind such fortresses a few men could hold off an army.

Quickly analyzing the situation, the sheriff said, "Let 'em go, boys. They have the advantage now, but they can't stay up there long or go far without food, blankets, or horses."

The posse then returned to Bassett's ranch for the night, taking with them all of the outlaws' possessions.

From a rimrock cave on the side of the mountain Harry Tracy, David Lant, and P. L. Johnson watched the group leave. Tracy and Lant had escaped from the Utah penitentiary only a few months before and were hiding out in Brown's Park, where they had met Johnson and "Judge" Bennett. Tracy, Lant, and Johnson had come to the foot of Douglas Mountain to await Bennett, who had arranged to join his friends there with fresh provisions. Upon arriving at their rendezvous, Bennett was supposed to fire three shots in rapid succession for identification purposes.

"They were too yellow to shoot it out with us," Harry Tracy growled. He was small, dark, and vicious-looking.

"I don't blame 'em," David Lant said. "We could've picked off the whole bunch if they had started up the mountain." Lant was a big man with a kindlier face than his two companions.

"They'll be comin' back tomorrow," Johnson said. "Let's lite a shuck out of here." Johnson was a big Swede with the brutal eyes of a natural killer.

Early the next morning when Sheriff Neiman and his men returned to Douglas Mountain they found the footprints of the outlaws going westward. The posse, traveling much faster on horseback, followed the fresh tracks to Green River, where they led into Lodore Canyon.

Unable to scale the steep west walls of the canyon and make their escape into Utah as planned, the outlaws had proceeded down the frozen river until it narrowed between the canyon walls into a roaring cataract, which prevented the formation of ice. Exhausted, cold, and discouraged, the hunted men returned to their former retreat on Douglas Mountain in the same rimrock cave they had occupied the previous evening. Then, deciding to look for a better fortress, they continued some distance farther up the mountain.

The posse, in the meantime, followed the fugitives' tracks down Green River to the cataract and back again. Upon arriving at Douglas Mountain the small, hardy sheriff was faced with the same difficult problem that he had encountered the evening before. While outnumbered three to one, the bandits were in a position to hold off a much greater number from whatever cave or rock on the precipitous slope that they might have chosen to make their stand. They had all the high cards in case the posse decided to shoot it out with them on the mountainside.

On the other hand, a waiting game was all to the advantage of the sheriff and his deputies. The outlaws were without food, blankets, coats, or horses, and the great canyons to the south and west cut off escape in every direction except north or east, where they would sooner or later be forced to go in search of food.

The sheriff realized all of this, but his men were impatient. There had been much grumbling on the previous day when he had persuaded them to return to the Bassett ranch for the night without any attempt to arrest the outlaws. To repeat the same course again might cause most of the posse to give up the chase. So, for the sake of morale, Neiman decided to go up Douglas Mountain after the outlaws in spite of the odds.

The men dismounted, and the horses were left in charge of two men, who were warned to be on guard against the bandits doubling back on their trail and trying to escape on the mounts of their pursuers. The sheriff also stationed Eb Bassett and Boyd Vaughn where they could keep a lookout over the lower country in case of an attempted get-away in that direction.

Then Sheriff Neiman, Undersheriff Farnham, and three others took the most dangerous assignment and followed the fresh tracks up the mountain.

Footprints led up a narrow draw which in places was so steep that the officers had to grasp hold of trees and rocks in order to pull themselves forward.

As the little group worked themselves cautiously upward from tree to tree and rock to rock, they came to a gigantic boulder which was split by a crack just wide enough for a man to crawl through.

The posse stopped for a time just below this split rock to inspect a camping site where the fugitives had built a fire, mixed snow with some flour, the only food apparently in their possession, and baked the mixture on hot coals.

While the others were examining this campground, Valentine Hoy, a pioneer cattle rancher of Brown's Park, walked on ahead about twenty feet to the crevice in the monstrous rock. As he approached, two rifle reports echoed over the mountain, and Hoy fell dead in the snow.

His four companions ran for the protection of the nearest rocks. Tracy's tense face peered through the crack in search of another target. Neiman pulled up his rifle, but the outlaw ducked back before he could shoot. Neiman and Tracy were so close to one another during that fleeting moment that the next time they met each recognized the other.

The bandits were in complete command of the situation. The five members of the posse were cornered behind two rocks just a few feet apart. They could not advance or circle around the three outlaws without exposing themselves to certain death. So, admitting temporary defeat, one man at a time crawled back down the slope while the others kept the big rock covered.

During these developments Boyd Vaughn and Eb Bassett were maintaining their watch over the lower country. While at their posts they espied a horseman in the distance. He rode up to a prominent point at the foot of the mountain, and drawing a six-shooter from his holster, fired three shots in rapid succession. He waited a long time as if expecting an answer. When nothing happened, he fired three more times with his rifle.

Vaughn and Bassett mounted their horses and rode toward the newcomer. When they neared the rider, Basset recognized him as "Judge" Bennett, who apparently was bringing provisions to the three men in hiding.

Bennett was surprised to see the two horsemen, but since he was well acquainted with Bassett, he suspected nothing. Bassett invited Bennett to ride back with him and spend the night at his ranch. Bennett accepted, and the two men rode away together while Vaughn went in a different direction on the pretext of looking for stray cattle.

As soon as Vaughn was out of sight, he spurred his horse and galloped away to notify the sheriff. Sheriff Neiman and his men had all reached the foot of the mountain when Vaughn rode up. When told that Bennett was on his way to Bassett's ranch, the posse took a different route and rode hard to get there before the outlaw did. Bennett's horse was tired from his long journey and traveled slowly, which enabled the sheriff and his men to reach the ranch first.

Bennett's horse was traveling so slowly when the "Judge" and Bassett neared the ranch that Bassett rode on ahead. The sheriff instructed him to accompany the outlaw from the barn to the back door and then allow Bennett to enter first so that the men stationed inside could grab him. Bassett did as requested, and Bennett was taken prisoner. The sheriff put shackles on his hands and ankles and removed two revolvers from their holsters.

On the following day Undersheriff Farnham remained at the ranch to guard the prisoner, who was being confined in the bunk house, while the rest of the posse resumed the manhunt.

Bennett lay on a bunk with his feet and hands in shackles. The undersheriff sat in a chair near the door facing the prisoner. Farnham was reading a book when the door unexpectedly opened. A group of masked men entered and covered him with their six-shooters.

"Now, all you have to do is keep quiet," one of them warned in a low voice.

Other men, also wearing masks, came into the bunk house carrying a burlap sack. They put it over the surprised prisoner's head and carried him out of the room. Several of the group stayed with Farnham for about ten minutes.

"We'll leave," one of the masked men said finally, "if you give us your word not to leave this room for thirty minutes."

"All right," the undersheriff agreed. "There ain't much else I can do."

After the allotted time had passed, Farnham opened the door and peered out into the cold quiet day. The cattle rustler, his face hidden by the gunnysack, was swinging at the end of a rope tied to a high cross-bar over the corral gate.

That evening posses from Wyoming and Utah joined the Colorado group at the Bassett ranch to participate in

the hunt. Wyoming officials had been notified that Johnson, the killer of William Strang, was hiding in Brown's
Park; and Utah officials had come for Lant and Tracy,
who had escaped from the Utah penitentiary.

The next morning the posses discovered the outlaws'
tracks going north across the mail road.

"They're probably headed for one of the three sheep
camps just over the Wyoming line," Sheriff Neiman commented.

So, he divided his forces into three parties, each to take
the shortest route to one of the sheep camps. A fourth
group, composed of E. B. "Longhorn" Thompson of
Brown's Park and Pete Dillman and Jerry Murray of Wyoming, followed the tracks.[6]

The fugitives were undoubtedly exhausted, frozen, and
nearly starved. They were without coats, and the tracks
showed that their worn-out shoes had been wrapped with
cloth torn from their clothes.

"Longhorn" Thompson and Pete Dillman took the
lead while Jerry Murray came along behind, driving the
pack horses. As they were following the tracks through a
grove of trees, Murray broke off a dead branch and tossed
it at one of the pack horses.

"Quit makin' so much noise," Thompson snapped.
"Them outlaws might hear you."

The quick-tempered Murray spurred his horse up to
Thompson and put his hand on the butt of his six-shooter.
"If you don't like the way I'm drivin' them horses, drive
'em yourself, you cowardly son of a bitch."[7]

"Here, boys," Dillman exclaimed, "we're here to catch outlaws, not to fight among ourselves."

After this exchange of words, "Longhorn" Thompson dropped back and drove the pack horses.

During the noon hour Thompson remarked, "We're really gonna have a battle on our hands when we catch up with them outlaws."

"Hell, no," Dillman disagreed. "They're cold, starved, and worn out. They won't have no fight left in 'em."

In the meantime, Undersheriff Farnham and three other Colorado cowboys arrived at the site of one of the sheep camps just across the Wyoming line. The camp, however, was abandoned, and the party was just getting ready to follow the wagon tracks when they saw the three men approaching. Hiding in the cedars, the posse waited.

The outlaws walked up to the deserted camp and kicked around in the snow for some scraps of food that the sheepherders might have left.

"Hands up!" Farnham's voice rang out.

Startled, the outlaws started to run with bullets hitting all around them. In their weakened condition they kept stumbling and falling down in the snow. Each time the posse thought that the fleeing bandits had been killed, they would struggle to their feet and stagger on.[8]

One bullet passed between Johnson's legs, kicking up snow in front of him. He threw up his hands and walked back toward the cowboys, who took him prisoner.

Lant and Tracy jumped into a gulch partly filled with snow, and were preparing to make a stand when the Wyoming posse and the three men who had been following the outlaws' tracks arrived on the scene.[9]

"Boys," Sheriff William Preece of Wyoming shouted, "you might just as well give up or we'll have to kill you."

Hopelessly outnumbered, the outlaws argued between themselves.

Suddenly Lant crawled up into view.

"Come back here, you son of a bitch," Tracy yelled to his comrade, "or I'll blow your head off."

Lant rolled back into the wash to argue some more. Before long he again appeared, and without any interference this time he gave himself up.

"You bastards will never take me alive," Tracy called out, a tinge of hatred in his voice.

"You ain't got a chance," Undersheriff Farnham yelled back. "We can starve you out."

There was a moment's silence.

"Sheriff," Tracy answered finally, "if you'll promise me a fair trial, I'll give myself up."

"Agreed," Farnham shouted. "Now you're bein' sensible." The undersheriff breathed a sigh of relief as Tracy stumbled forward with his hands in the air.

Tracy and Johnson were carrying Winchesters, and all three of the fugitives had revolvers. These were taken away from them, and the prisoners were escorted to Bassett's ranch.[10] They were shackled and put in the bunk house where two men from the three posses, consisting of around 60 men, alternated in keeping a continual guard during the night. Several movements were started by hot-heads to lynch the three prisoners, but each time Sheriff Neiman talked them out of it.

The next morning Johnson was taken to Wyoming by the Wyoming posse for the killing of Willie Strang. For some reason he was acquitted at the trial. He was then brought to Routt County to stand trial for being an accessory to the murder of Valentine Hoy on Douglas Mountain. He claimed that Tracy shot Hoy over his protests. Nevertheless, he was found guilty of second degree murder and sentenced to the state penitentiary for ten to fifteen years.

Tracy and Lant were put in the Routt County jail at the town of Hahns Peak, twenty-five miles north of Steamboat Springs, by the Colorado posse for the murder of Valentine Hoy; and the Utah posse returned home empty-handed.

Sheriff Neiman personally looked after Lant and Tracy, who were confined in one cell of the small log jail. Most of the time, however, they were also allowed the use of the corridor. When someone entered the jail to bring meals or for other purposes, Lant and Tracy would enter their cell from the corridor, pull the door shut, and a lever was thrown from outside the corridor by the attendant to bolt the cell door. Then the door to the corridor, which had a separate lock, was unlocked with a key and the meal brought in and placed in the corridor. After going back out, the attendant would lock the corridor door and unbolt the cell door so that the two prisoners could go out into the corridor to eat.

One evening when the sheriff went in to remove the

This picture of Harry Tracy was taken at the Oregon penitentiary in 1899. *Photo courtesy of Denver Public Library Western Collection.*

dishes, the prisoners, as usual, started for their cell from
the corridor, where they had been walking. It was growing
dark, and the outlaws had purposely broken the lamp chim-
ney and taken it off the lamp in order to make the light
dim.

Lant, who was in his stocking feet, walked in first.
Tracy, who was following, suddenly turned and said,
"Sheriff, could you lend me a match?"

Neiman reached into his pocket as Tracy sauntered
over to the door of the corridor.

"Much obliged," the prisoner said, accepting the match
through the bars of the door.

In that instant when the sheriff looked away from Lant
to hand Tracy the match, Lant, panther-like, stepped
quickly into an adjoining cell, the door of which was open.

After receiving the match Tracy walked into his cell
and closed the door. Neiman then proceeded to bolt it,
assuming that Lant was in there too.

Unlocking the door to the corridor, the sheriff entered
to gather up the dishes. As he did so, Lant charged the
smaller man with his head down. After a short fight the
battered sheriff lay still, feigning unconsciousness, since he
was no match for the big outlaw.

Lant pocketed the keys which were in the open door,
and grasping the lever, unbolted the cell door. Tracy
stepped out with a snarl and gave the reclining officer a
vigorous kick. He then kneeled down and placed his ear
against the sheriff's chest.

"His heart is beatin' awful strong, Dave," he commented. "Let's kill the bastard."

"You don't need to worry about him," Lant said. "He's safe enough."

They carried the sheriff into the cell and laid him on the bunk. They searched him for a gun but were disappointed to find that the officer was unarmed. Keeping the personal effects that Neiman was carrying, which consisted of a watch and pocketbook, the outlaws bound and gagged him.

They waited an hour longer until it was dark and then departed, locking the door and lever and taking the jail keys with them. It was twenty-eight degrees below zero, and the two men were without coats, overshoes, or gloves. They made their way through the snow to the livery stable where the tired stage team were eating hay after just recently arriving from Steamboat Springs. They untied the steaming horses, replaced the bridles, and led them out into the cold, moonlight night. Jumping on them bareback, the outlaws started down the road toward Steamboat Springs.

Twice they had to stop and waste precious time building fires in order to keep from freezing to death. They finally reached Steamboat Springs an hour before daylight. With difficulty they urged their exhausted mounts through the sleeping village. As they passed the door of the stage barn, the horses tried to turn in.

After riding out of town they continued along the stage road to the W. J. Laramore ranch, which was situated a few miles south of town. Knocking at the door of the ranch house, they were greeted by Laramore, who was eating breakfast. They told the rancher that they were cattlemen who had to make an emergency trip to the railroad. They asked permission to leave their horses at Laramore's ranch and wait for the stage, which would be along shortly on its way to the nearest railroad station at Wolcott. The rancher accepted their unusual story without question and invited the frozen strangers to have breakfast with him.

While all this was going on, Sheriff Neiman and a posse were in hot pursuit. A short time after the outlaws had escaped, the sheriff managed to attract the attention of a passer-by who found the officer lying tied and gagged in his own jail. A pewter key, found on a recent inmate who had designed it after the original, was located in the sheriff's room and used to unlock the corridor. However, there was no duplicate key to the lever which bolted the cell doors; so sledges and chisels were used by the townspeople to force open the door to the cell where Neiman was lying.

Still groggy from his terrible beating, the hardy little sheriff organized a posse and started out after his escaped prisoners. In the moonlight the riders had no difficulty following the fresh horse tracks along the road to Steamboat Springs. Although Tracy and Lant had a two-hour start, their draft horses were slow travelers, and much time was lost in building fires to warm themselves. They did not hurry, believing that the sheriff would not regain consciousness until daylight.

The posse rode into Steamboat Springs just an hour behind the outlaws. Neiman sent riders along all roads leading out of town. Suspecting that the fugitives might try to catch the stage sleigh for Wolcott, the sheriff and a deputy went along in it, bundled in heavy fur overcoats which made recognition difficult.

The stage was hailed at the Laramore ranch, and the driver turned into the side road. Still wearing no coats or gloves in the sub-zero weather, Lant and Tracy walked over to the sleigh. Just before they got in, the sheriff and his deputy covered the surprised outlaws with six-shooters and ordered them to put up their hands.

"Hello, Neiman," Tracy said as he complied with the request, "I thought you would just be waking up."

The officers got out of the stage, and borrowing a sleigh and team from Laramore, they took their prisoners back to Steamboat Springs. When they pulled into town, Neiman stopped at the Adair Hardware to procure a log chain and two padlocks. The outlaws were kept under guard in the office of the Sheridan Hotel while the posse from Hahns Peak had breakfast. Armed guards stood in the doorways to prevent the prisoners from escaping and to keep back the curious crowds which tried to get a look at the captured bandits.

Before returning to Hahns Peak, the sheriff chained the prisoners together by their necks and fastened an Oregon boot, or a heavy weight, on the ankle of each. These Oregon boots were left on the outlaws after they were again placed in their old quarters in the Routt County jail.

Lant and Tracy took advantage of the occasion by sleeping all day and pounding their Oregon boots against the steel bars of their cells all night long. After the residents of Hahns Peak could stand the nightly commotion no longer, Sheriff Neiman took the matter up with Judge

Thomas A. Rucker. On April 1, 1898, Judge Rucker ordered the removal of the troublesome captives to the Aspen jail in Pitkin County to await trial.

Although better constructed, the jail at Aspen had the same type of locks as the one at Hahns Peak. One day a few weeks after the removal of the prisoners, the jailer came to get the dinner dishes, which were sitting on a table in the corridor.

Lant and Tracy walked into their cell and slammed the door shut. Then, quick as a cat, one of them noiselessly opened it a trifle. The jailer yanked on the lever to throw in the bolt which failed to catch in the open door. The attendant then unlocked the corridor door and entered. As he started to pick up the dishes, the two prisoners threw open their cell door and jumped on him. After nearly beating the jailer to death, they made their escape in broad daylight.

Lant was never heard of again, but the vicious, cold-blooded Tracy made the headlines some months later when he escaped from a penitentiary in a northwestern state, and in a period of two weeks killed eight officers before turning his gun on himself when finally cornered. A fitting reward for a life of crime.

FOOTNOTES

[1]Most of the material for this story was obtained from J. S. Hoy, "The History of Brown's Park," C.W.A. Interviews, 1933-34, Moffat County, pp. 107-117.

[2]So-called because as one of a drunken band of outlaws in southern Wyoming Bennett presided over a kangaroo court

which tried a kidnapped physician after he had unsuccessfully treated a member of the gang who died of pneumonia. Before the hanging some other wild escapade attracted the attention of the drunken outlaws, and the doctor was allowed to go free.

[3]J. Monaghan, "Report on Fort David Crockett," C.W.A. Interviews, Moffat Co., 1933-34, p. 127.

[4]Douglas Mountain was named after Chief Douglas of the Utes, who spent many summers during the reservation years in Colo. camped at the foot of it. Douglas was one of the chief instigators of the Meeker massacre.

[5]*Craig Courier,* March 5, 1898.

[6]Pete Dillman, C.W.A. Interviews, Moffat Co., 1933-34, p. 42. In possession of the State Historical Society of Colorado.

[7]*Ibid.*

[8]*Ibid.*

[9]*Ibid.*

[10]Hoy, *op. cit*

Durango, Colorado, in 1881. The tree to which gambler Moorman was hanged is in center of picture. *Photo courtesy of Denver Public Library Western Collection.*

# X

## THE BETRAYAL

Three cowboys swung off their horses and tied them up at one of the hitching posts in front of the lighted cabin of F. M. Hamlet, about four miles from Farmington, New Mexico. It was Christmas Eve, 1880, and the muffled sound of laughter, music and stamping feet could be heard inside the dwelling.

The three newcomers, talking boisterously and drunkenly, staggered up to the door and knocked. The door was opened, revealing a Christmas Eve party in full swing.

The host's face sobered when he saw that the uninvited guests were Dyson Eskridge, James Garrett, and Oscar Pruett, members of the Stockton-Eskridge gang of Durango, Colorado, who were feuding with the Frank Simmons cattle outfit of Farmington.

Each side had been accusing the other of rustling cattle, and the two groups of rival cattlemen had accumulated a formidable array of gunmen to represent their respective interests. Dow Eskridge was owner of the Eskridge ranch near Durango, but his younger, more reckless brothers, Harg and Dyson, actually ran the gang until Ike Stockton, the celebrated killer, rode in from Texas and threw in his lot with the Eskridges. From that time on he was recognized as the leader with Harg and Dyson Eskridge second and third in command.[1]

Although none of the Simmons gang was at the party, Hamlet hesitated about allowing the three cowboys inside since the people of Farmington generally sympathized with the local group and disliked the Stockton-Eskridge band. But, after all, Hamlet considered, it was Christmas Eve— a time to be hospitable even to one's enemies.

"Ain't you going to let us in, Ham?" Dyson Eskridge asked, noticing Hamlet's indecision.

"Sure," Hamlet answered, stepping aside. "How are you, Dice? The last time I seen you was in the Grand Central Hotel at Durango."

"I don't remember the occasion," Dyson said as he and his unshaven comrades strode into the house, spurs jingling.

"Well, you wasn't there long. You rode your horse into the barroom and stayed just long enough to shoot up the place. You might have stayed longer, but Marshal Bob Dwyer relieved you of your guns."[2]

His mind befogged with whiskey, Dyson took his host's pleasantries as a reflection on his courage. "I ain't afraid of Bob Dwyer," he grumbled. "He asked me for my guns, and I gave them to him. He was very friendly about it."

"Yeah, Dwyer's got a cool head all right. By the way, boys, you'll have to remove your guns while you're in the house, like the other fellows have done. I'll put them in the bedroom until you're ready to leave. They'll be waitin' for you."

Arrival of the three desperadoes put a damper on the gaiety and general good feeling. The newcomers talked so loudly and profanely that Hamlet finally handed them their guns and requested them to leave.

They rebuckled on their holsters and stumbled out into the yard, where they began yelling and shooting off their revolvers into the air.

Hamlet went to the doorway. "Dice, you'd better take your men and get out of here pronto. We've got you outnumbered. Move on now."

"We just wanted to return a little of your Christmas cheer," Dyson Eskridge shouted, firing at the house. His companions followed suit, and one of the shots hit and killed George Brown who was standing beside Hamlet. As the volley of bullets cracked into the house, the men inside ran out and returned the fire as the horsemen galloped away.[3]

The town of Farmington was highly incensed at this latest outrage by members of the Stockton-Eskridge gang. A reward of one thousand dollars was offered for their capture, dead or alive, preferably dead, and a posse of seventeen men was quickly organized.

The three fugitives left the country for several months until the affair quieted down, and then they appeared in

Durango, which was headquarters for the Stockton-Esk-ridge band.

When the people of Farmington learned about the re-turn of Dyson Eskridge and his two followers to Durango, they organized another posse of about fifty men to capture the entire gang and bring them back to Farmington to stand trial for murder and cattle rustling.

The posse rode into Durango Sunday evening on April 11, 1881.[4] Although the town had just been founded the preceding fall, it was already a flourishing community of 2,500 people. Among its 150 business houses were six dry goods stores, three drug stores, one bank, one variety the-ater, six hotels, three newspapers, ten restaurants, and twenty saloons.[5] The mayor and other city officials had not yet been elected, and the six-month old town was wide open.

The Farmington posse was surprised to find a corpse swinging by the neck from a large pine tree in front of the post office. Durango's first lynching had been per-formed by its hastily organized Committee of Safety, com-posed of some 300 masked men. Armed men of the com-mittee were still patrolling the streets and warning curious crowds of spectators not to cut down the body under pen-alty of death.

The man who hung from the tree was Henry Moor-man, a gambler at the Coliseum, who that morning had shot and killed James Prindle. At eleven o'clock the Com-mittee of Safety had escorted the killer to the large pine tree, where the execution took place.

The men from Farmington decided that conditions

were too hot in Durango to start a fight with the Stockton-Eskridge gang. So they rode on up to Animas City, three miles distant, for the night, hoping that by the following day they could accomplish their mission without interference from the aroused citizens of Durango. When they discovered the next morning that the Committee of Safety was still very much on the job, the posse wisely started back to Farmington.

As the horsemen were crossing the mesa just east of Durango, some of the Stockton-Eskridge gang recognized them from the saloons on Railroad Street. Running outside, they shot up toward the riders. The posse jumped off their horses and returned the fire.

The skirmish lasted for nearly an hour before the Farmington group continued on their way. Bullets whistled through the streets and houses of Durango, wounding two bystanders.

At the first sound of the shooting, A. P. Camp peeked out the door of the First National Bank Building where he was cashier. Upon seeing the commotion, he immediately hid the money and closed up the bank.

Stray bullets crashed into the brand new West End Hotel, later called the Leland Hotel, which had scheduled a big opening dinner and ball for that evening.[6] The grand opening was postponed for two weeks while the damage was repaired and the town quieted down.

One bullet passed through the *Durango Record* building, badly frightening its lady editor and publisher, Mrs. C. W. Romney.[7] In the next issue she wrote an indignant editorial demanding that the citizens call a general

meeting to decide on the best means of getting rid of the
Stockton-Eskridge gang whom she described as a menace
to the community.

Shortly after the editorial appeared, Ike Stockton and
Harg Eskridge payed a visit to the newspaper office and
asked to see the editor. They were surprised to discover
that the editor was a woman.

"If you were a man," Ike Stockton said in his usual
quiet, forceful manner, "we would make you retract that
piece you wrote, but since you're a woman, we will just ask
you to do it and try to explain our side."

"No explanations are necessary," Mrs. Romney said,
quaking in her shoes. "There will be no apologies or re-
tractions."

"All right then, lady, be prepared to take the consequences."

A guard was placed around the newspaper building,
and for the next ten days the printers carried revolvers
while they worked. A dozen loaded rifles were placed in
convenient corners of the composing room, ready for instant action. However, the Committee of Safety had not
disbanded, and for once the Stockton-Eskridge gang was
afraid to start anything.

Aroused by the shooting and the editorial, the townspeople of Durango had a meeting and drafted a resolution
notifying the gang to get out of Durango. The group complied since they were afraid that if they refused they would
be arrested and turned over to the Farmington officials.

The band next established Rico as their headquarters,
where the people were more friendly to them. In fact, for

a long time the editors of the *Dolores News*—Clifford Jones and Frank Hartman—had championed the Stockton-Eskridge cause against the Frank Simmons band of Farmington.

In May, 1881, about a month after the Durango gun battle, Governor Lew Wallace of New Mexico issued a proclamation offering rewards for members of the Stockton-Eskridge gang. Clifford Jones replied by composing a letter to the governor for Ike Stockton and Harg Eskridge to sign. It read:

> Rico, Colo.
> May 26, 1881

To His Excellency the Governor of New Mexico:

Inasmuch as you have made requisitions on Frederick W. Pitkin as Governor of Colorado for the undersigned, we beg leave to state to you the exact position in which we are placed.

We have never committed a crime against the laws of the United States, of Colorado, or of New Mexico, the public press and current rumor to the contrary notwithstanding. Said requisitions were obtained by misrepresentation and perjury of men who have sworn to kill us. These men belong to an organized band, with whose depredations and murder you should be tolerably familiar. . . .

> Yours very respectfully,
> I. T. Stockton
> J. H. Eskridge[8]

Bert Wilkinson, an overgrown, likeable boy, who occasionally did the janitor work at the *Dolores News,* was a member of the gang and had risked his life many times for the Stockton-Eskridge cause.[9]

In August, 1881, a negro, known as Kid Thomas, rode
into Rico. He worked at Fort Lewis as a cowboy, herding
cattle that were to be butchered each day for the soldiers
stationed there. Thomas's brother had been arrested for
robbing a stage near Conejos in the San Luis Valley.
Shortly before he was caught, he got word to Thomas that
he had hidden the loot.[10]

Kid Thomas got a ten-day vacation to go visit his
brother, who was to stand trial in Conejos. Upon arriving
in Rico the negro looked up Bert Wilkinson and Dyson
Eskridge, whom he had met in Durango while the Stockton-Eskridge gang was headquartering there. He told them
about the loot and asked them to accompany him to Conejos to find out from his brother where it was hidden.
Thomas felt that members of the notorious Stockton-Eskridge gang would be more experienced in such matters outside the law. As an added inducement to Eskridge and
Wilkinson, he divided equally the $300 salary that he had
received just before leaving Fort Lewis.

The three men stopped for the night in Silverton on
their way to Conejos. They intended to approach Conejos from the north, thereby avoiding the regular run of
travelers between Durango and the San Luis Valley. While
at Silverton they stopped in a dance hall for some drinks.

After a time Dyson Eskridge got that familiar gleam in
his eyes and ran true to form by shooting at the lights. Wilkinson joined in the fun, but Thomas, who was drinking
more moderately, did not participate.

Clate Ogsbury, the Silverton marshal, hurried into the
dance hall. As he came through the door, one of the flying

bullets killed him. Wilkinson and Eskridge ran out the back entrance and escaped on foot into the mountains.

The sheriff assembled a posse of twenty-four men and went after the killers. The negro, who had taken no part in the shooting, made no effort to get away. He was arrested and placed in jail. The next night a mob broke into the jail and escorted Kid Thomas to the court house shed, where they hung him to a cross-beam.[11]

Wilkinson and Eskridge made their way to a small, out-of-the-way stage station at Castle Rock on the road from Rockwood to Rico. A former Rico man, who was a friend of the two fugitives, was in charge of the place. He was away at the time, but his wife hid the men in a canyon some distance away from the house and brought them food each night.[12] When the Castle Rock station and buildings were searched by the San Juan County sheriff and his posse, no trace of Wilkinson and Eskridge was found.

The popular Silverton marshal was buried on August 26, 1881, two days after he was killed, and the funeral was the largest ever held in that town.

In their anxiety to get hold of the killers, the people of Silverton offered a formidable reward of $2500 for each of the pursued men. As soon as Ike Stockton heard about the shooting and the reward, he rode out of Rico in search of his friends.

He knew that the proprietor of the Castle Rock station was friendly to him and his gang; so he suspected that Wilkinson and Eskridge were hiding out somewhere in that vicinity. Upon arriving at Castle Rock, Stockton told the proprietor's wife that he had come to help the boys escape. Since Stockton was their leader, she naturally supposed that he was sincere. Consequently, she took Stockton to their hideout in the canyon.

The three men borrowed some extra horses and started south. When they arrived at La Plata Mesa, they stopped for a short rest while Stockton explained his plan for their getaway. He told Dyson Eskridge to ride to George Morrison's ranch on the Los Pinos to get five extra mounts and then meet him and Wilkinson at a designated place, from which the two fugitives would ride on to Old Mexico.

The next morning after Eskridge had left, Stockton pulled out his six-shooter and covered Wilkinson, whose gun and holster lay on his blankets just a few feet out of reach.

"Throw up your hands, Bert. You're my prisoner!"

Wilkinson glanced at the older man with a puzzled smile, "Now, that ain't very damn funny, Ike. Remember, I've got the jitters."

"I ain't kiddin' yuh, Bert," Stockton said, taking charge of Wilkinson's six-shooter. "I hate to turn yuh in, but I need that reward money awful bad."

"Why, you double crossin' son of a bitch," Wilkinson exclaimed as the truth suddenly dawned upon him. "I suppose you let Dice go on account of his brother Harg, but you'll find that I've got friends too."

Upon reaching Animas City, Stockton sent word to the San Juan County sheriff that he had captured Wilkinson and would turn him over to the proper authorities if they would bring the reward and come to Animas City to get him. The sheriff, fearing that Stockton and his gang intended to rescue Wilkinson after being paid the $2500, replied by a return messenger that the reward would not be paid until delivery of the prisoner in Silverton.

Stockton agreed to do so if the sheriff would furnish him with a protecting escort out of town. Stockton was taking no chances with the enraged citizens of that area, who associated the killing with his gang.

Stockton delivered his prisoner, received the money, and was escorted out of town.

"Now you are on your own, Ike," the sheriff said. "And I advise you to make yourself scarce because the people around here don't like double crossers."

Jim Sullivan, deputy sheriff of La Plata County, happened to be in town when Wilkinson was put in the Silverton jail. Sullivan was acquainted with the prisoner; so, accompanied by Andy Chitwood, he dropped around to see the boy.

Wilkinson told them all about the betrayal. Before his friends left, he said, "I didn't shoot the marshal.[13] I can prove it if I get a fair trial."

"You're in a pretty tough spot, Bert," Sullivan said frankly. "The people around here are really on the prod. They lynched Kid Thomas, and not a cartridge in his gun had been fired."

"I know I ain't got a chance, Jim, but before I die, I just wish I could get one last shot at Ike Stockton."

"I've always been a friend of Ike's until now," Sullivan said bitterly. "But I promise you that if things work out so that you can't get that last shot, I'll take it for you."[14]

Wilkinson poked his hand through the bars and grasped the deputy's hand tightly.

"I wonder if you'd do me one more favor, Jim."

"I sure will, kid."

"Write my family in Farmington and tell them that I didn't kill the marshal."

That night the San Juan County sheriff was over-powered, and a mob of masked men took Wilkinson out to the court house shed where Kid Thomas had been lynched. The victim was asked to step on a chair, and a rope was tied around his neck and made fast to a rafter.

Ending any further ceremony or action by the mob, Wilkinson cried out, "Adios, gentlemen!"

As he spoke, he kicked the chair from under his feet and dangled in the air.[15]

Deputy Sheriff Jim Sullivan of La Plata County knew of several unlawful acts that Ike Stockton had committed at one time in Cook County, Texas. So, he sent to Gainesville for a warrant. Sullivan knew that Stockton would probably shoot it out with him before submitting to arrest.

Upon receiving the warrant, the deputy walked around the streets of Durango until he found Stockton. As the two men approached each other, Sullivan said, "Ike, I've got a warrant for your arrest."

As he spoke, Sullivan pulled out the warrant with one hand and his forty-five with the other.

Stockton's trained hand grasped for his gun, but he drew a fraction of a second too late. His bullet blasted a hole in the sidewalk as he fell with a slug in his thigh bone. The femoral artery had been severed, and he was taken over to the San Juan smelter where efforts were made to stop the bleeding.

A crowd of bystanders assembled outside the door, and as the wounded gunman bled to death, they shouted the refrain, "Go to hell and face Bert Wilkinson!"

Jim Sullivan had kept his promise.[16]

FOOTNOTES

[1]Charles A. Jones, "The Lynching of Bert Wilkinson," *Pioneers of the San Juan,* Vol. 3 by Sarah Platt Decker Chapter, D.A.R., Durango Printing Co., Durango, Colo., 1952, p. 68.

[2]George Doughty, acct., LaPlata Co., C.W.A. Workers Interviews, collected for the State Historical Society, 1933-34, p. 31. In possession of the State Historical Society of Colorado.

[3]*The Durango Record,* Jan. 10, 1881.

[4]Mary C. Ayres, "The Founding of Durango," *The Colorado Magazine,* May, 1930, p. 91.

[5]Florence Wilson Netherton, "Durango's First Newspaper," *Pioneers of the San Juan Country,* Vol. 2, D.A.R., Durango, Colo., 1946, p. 22.

[6]*The Durango Record,* April 9, 1881.

[7]Ayres, *op. cit.,* p. 91.

[8]*Dolores News,* May 25, 1881.

[9]Jones, *op. cit.,* p. 72.

[10]George E. West, "The Oldest Range Man," *Pioneers of the San Juan* by Sarah Platt Decker Chapter, D.A.R., Vol. 2, pp. 117-118.

[11]West, *op. cit.,* p. 118.

[12]Jones, *op. cit.,* p. 73.

[13]Jones, *op. cit.,* p. 76.

[14]Doughty, *op. cit.,* p. 31.

[15]Jones, *op. cit.,* p. 74.

[16]Dyson Eskridge, assisted by his brother Harg, got out of the country and was never arrested. With the leaders gone, the notorious Stockton-Eskridge gang quickly fell apart.

Port Stockton, Ike Stockton's brother, was also killed in a shooting scrape. In 1880 Port Stockton was marshal of Animas City. One day while being shaved by a high-strung, colored barber, the barber accidentally cut him.

"If you cut me again, I'll kill you," the marshal warned.

This made the negro all the more nervous, and it wasn't long before he nicked the gunman again. Port started to get to his feet and the barber took to his heels. With a bloody face and the towel still wrapped around his neck, Port chased the barber down the street, shooting as he ran. One of the bullets cut a big gash in the barber's head. The negro, still wearing his apron, sought refuge in the shop of Charles Naeglin.

Eugene Engley, editor of *The Southwest* newspaper of Animas City and mayor of the town, deputized Naeglin to help him arrest Port Stockton. They found the marshal and placed him under arrest. Port asked if he might be allowed to go home for supper before being lodged in jail. Engley consented and accompanied him. While Engley watched the door, Stockton crawled out a window and made his escape on a horse which happened to be tied nearby.

Port later showed up around Farmington, where he jumped a homestead claim. The owner was in Lake City to record his claim. After returning, he shot it out with Stockton and was killed. The dead man's wife reported the incident, and a posse went after Stockton, killing him in a gun battle.

# XI

# THE MEEKER MASSACRE

Nathan C. Meeker was a tall, thin man with a pleasing personality to casual acquaintances.[1] He was well-known as a poet before the Civil War. During the war he served as a correspondent for the New York *Tribune,* and after the war Horace Greeley, editor of the *Tribune,* sent him West. The letters Meeker wrote about his travels were featured in the newspaper.[2]

While in Colorado Meeker was much impressed with the Pikes Peak region, and when he returned to New York, he suggested to Greeley that they colonize this area. Greeley agreed to help and solicited subscriptions in the *Tribune* for the enterprise. Before long $10,000 was raised, and in 1870 Meeker set out for Colorado to found a colony.[3] Instead of locating near Pikes Peak as originally planned, he established his colony one hundred miles north on the Cache La Poudre River where more land could be irrigated. The newly founded town was named Greeley and became Colorado's most famous colony.

Although Meeker's colonizing venture proved a success, it was not a money-maker. So, when Meeker was offered the job of Indian agent for the Northern Utes at the White River Agency, he gladly accepted. Because of his outstanding background as a journalist and colonizer, much was expected of him.

Meeker arrived at his post on May 15, 1878, and entered enthusiastically into his duties. However, in spite of his high moral character, outstanding background, and pleasant manner, events proved that he had only a slight understanding of Indians and little ability to manage them.

His first major move to reform and civilize the Utes was moving the agency some fifteen miles to a new location in Powell's Valley about four-and-a-half miles down the White River from the present site of Meeker. This valley was in a more favorable location for agricultural pursuits, which the agent had made an important part of his program. The Indians had been pasturing their horses on the lush grass of Powell's Valley and were very much opposed to fencing and plowing up the area.[4]

One faction of the Northern Utes under the leadership of Captain Jack, a Ute chief with the tall, lithe figure of an Arapahoe, refused to move to the newly established site of the agency. The other faction, led by Chief Douglass, a short, chunky man with a sparse mustache, which was rare among Indians, accompanied Meeker to Powell's Valley.

Since an irrigation ditch was needed for his farming

project, Meeker persuaded the reluctant Utes to spend $3,000 of their money for its constructiton. The Indians showed no enthusiasm for digging the canal, and only about fifteen of them stayed consistently with the work. The same unwillingness was noticed in building fences, grubbing, plowing, and planting.

In order to prevent the Utes from taking long excursions off their reservation, Meeker made a ruling that rations would be issued once a week and that the head of each family had to be present before his family could receive anything. This weekly attendance kept the Utes from taking their customary hunting trips and was very distasteful to them.[5]

The growing resentment against Meeker was aggravated by the government's shameful neglect in the delivery of annuities to the Utes.

In spite of many warning signals, Meeker kept right on with his unpopular policies. During the summer of 1879 he had another eighty acres of land fenced, plowed, and irrigated. Again in early September he ordered some more plowing to be done.

A Ute by the name of Johnson, who had been somewhat of a favorite at the agency, unexpectedly became the ringleader of a group of Indians who started taking a firm stand against any more plowing. Johnson had 150 horses which grazed on the land Meeker was fencing and plowing, and the Indian didn't want any more of his pasture destroyed. He told the agent that he could continue the plowing on less desirable land, which was spotted with alkali. Meeker refused and told the plowman to proceed.

Josephine Meeker. *Photo courtesy State Historical Society of Colorado.*

Nathan C. Meeker. *Photo courtesy State Historical Society of Colorado.*

A few days later Johnson strode into Meeker's house and grabbed hold of the agent in the presence of Mrs. Meeker. Pushing Meeker outside, he gave him a terrific beating. Agency employees came to the victim's rescue before he was killed.

Meeker reported this incident to the Commissioner of Indian Affairs, and on September 15th the agent was notified that the War Department was sending Major T. T. Thornburg with two companies of infantry and two companies of cavalry to the White River Agency to furnish protection for the Meeker family and their employees.

On the morning of September 29, 1879, everything appeared calm and peaceful at the agency. At one o'clock that afternoon Meeker sent a message to Major Thornburg by Wilmer Eskridge. The note said:

> I expect to leave in the morning with Douglass and Serrick to meet you; things are peaceable, and Douglass flies the United States flag. If you have trouble in getting through the canyon today, let me know in what force. We have been on guard three nights and shall be tonight, not because we know there is danger but because there might be.[6]

Douglass seemed to be in a friendly mood when he talked with the agent that morning. He discussed the possibility of sending his son Frederick to school with Meeker's daughter, Josephine, and he accepted some food around noon that Mrs. Meeker gave him. Several other Utes also came to the agent's house around dinner time in hope of getting their usual handouts.[7]

Unbeknown to the people at the agency, Major Thornburg had been ambushed by Captain Jack and a large band of his followers about ten o'clock that morning.

After dinner the agency employees went about their respective duties. Arthur Thompson, Frank Dresser, and Shadrick Price resumed their work of putting a roof on a building. Thompson climbed on top, and Dresser and Price began pitching up dirt to him.[8] W. H. Post was carrying sacks of flour into one of the warehouses, and the other men were performing various tasks.

As Meeker's wife and his daughter Josephine were putting away the last of the dishes, they saw twenty or twenty-five Utes appear and begin shooting at the white men while they were at work. It was a little after one o'clock, and the Utes at the agency had just learned about Captain Jack's attack on Major Thornburg and his troops.

Most of the agency employees were killed before they could find shelter, but Frank Dresser, Mrs. Meeker, Josephine Meeker, and Mrs. Shadrick Price, wife of the agency's blacksmith, and her two children sought shelter in the milk house, which stood a short distance away from Meeker's home.

They remained there all afternoon listening to the intermittent shooting and activities of the Indians, but they were unable to see any of the horrors. The Utes set fire to several of the nearby buildings, and the smoke drifted into the milk house, making it difficult to breathe. When the smoke became unbearable, the frightened little group ran over to the agent's house. The Indians were too busy plundering and carrying off supplies to notice them.[9]

Realizing that the berserk savages would sooner or later come into the agent's headquarters, the survivors watched for an opportunity to make a get-away and hide in the surrounding territory. When they thought no one was watching, they made a dash for it, sprinting across the street and entering the plowed field north of the building where they had been hiding.

One of the Utes saw them, and in a few moments all of the Indians were in close pursuit, yelling and shouting. They easily caught up with the women and children, but Frank Dresser outran the pursuers. The Indians shot at him before giving up the chase. Mortally wounded, he crawled into a small cave to hide.

Mrs. Price, a buxom, good-looking young woman, was overtaken by three Indians whom she did not know. Her captors took her down to White River and placed her on a pile of blankets.

Mrs. Meeker was taken prisoner by a Ute whom she had never seen before who turned her over to Douglass, the leader of the massacre. As Douglass led her past her house, she asked if she might enter to get some medicine, a book, blankets, and a few other things. Douglass consented on the condition that she bring out all of the money she could find.

She went into the house followed by an Indian and returned with her equipment and thirty dollars which she handed to Douglass. Douglass kept twenty-six dollars and distributed four dollars in silver to the other Utes in the group.

When Mrs. Meeker passed the mutilated body of her

Douglass and Johnson. Johnson assaulted Nathan Meeker for plowing up his horse pasture. This attack caused Meeker to ask for the aid of troops which, in turn, precipitated the Thornburg ambush and Meeker massacre. Douglass was the leader in the Meeker massacre at the White River Agency. *Photo courtesy of State Historical Society of Colorado.*

husband lying on his back about two-hundred yards from the house, she started to kneel down and kiss him a last goodbye. However, noting the hatred on the faces of her captors, she was afraid to do so.

Josephine Meeker was taken prisoner by an Indian named Persune, who escorted her down to the bank of the river, where the other two women and Mrs. Price's two children were sitting on a pile of blankets.

After a time the women and children were put on horses and taken to a small canyon four or five miles distant where everyone dismounted. The Indians had been drinking continuously during the afternoon and many were intoxicated. They amused themselves by threatening the women with their guns and saying they were soldiers. Douglass drunkenly made fun of the way the guard had been kept at the agency.

A little later the party rode ten or twelve miles farther on to Douglass' camp from where they started southward to Mesa Creek in the Plateau Valley about thirty-five miles northeast of Grand Junction.

On October 11th General Wesley Merritt, who came to the rescue of Thornburg's command, arrived at the White River Agency. His most fearful expectations were realized. All of the buildings except the house that had been built for Johnson were burned down, and the site was one of utter desolation. The soldiers located all of the dead bodies of the victims.

The body of Wilmer Eskridge, who had left with Meeker's message to Thornburg just a few minutes before Douglass made his attack, was found two miles north of the agency. In a pocket was found the note written by Meeker which said that all was well at the agency and that he would meet Thornburg in the morning.[10]

Frank Dresser, who, although shot, had outrun the Utes in his dash for freedom, was found lying dead in a cave near the agency, his coat folded under his head for a pillow.

The body of Carl Goldstein, an itinerant Jew who was not in the employ of the agency, was found in a ditch some distance from the agency buildings. The body of another transient, Julius Moore, was also reported to have been found.

At the agency the naked, mutilated body of Nathan Meeker was found lying about two hundred yards from his house. One side of his head was bashed in, and a long barrel stave splinter had been driven through his mouth.[11]

Other bodies found were those of William Post, Harry Dresser, Albert Woodburn, Shadrick Price, who was the husband of the kidnapped woman, Arthur Thompson, Fred Shepard, and George Eaton.[12]

Mounds of earth were shoveled over the bodies where they lay. That fall they were removed by relatives.[13]

Edwin L. Mansfield was the only employee of the agency who escaped death. The reason for his good fortune was that three days before the massacre he had been sent with a dispatch to Captain F. S. Dodge in Middle Park.[14]

Charles Adams, an employe of the Post Office Department and a former agent at the Los Pinos Agency for the Uncompahgre Utes, was made a special agent on October 14, 1879, to recover the three women and two children who had been kidnapped by Douglass and his followers. Adams left Denver on October 15th and proceeded to the Uncompahgre Agency to get Chief Ouray's advice and help.[15]

On October 19th Adams started out to find Douglass' camp, which Ouray said was somewhere on Plateau Creek between the present towns of Palisade and DeBeque. He was accompanied by three Ute chiefs and two employees of the Uncompahgre Agency. In addititon to this official delegation, Count Von Doenhoff, a member of the German legation at Washington, became interested in the mission and went along as a spectator.[16] Adams carried orders from Ouray for immediate cessation of hostilities and for the surrender of the captives.

Two days later the little group arrived at Douglass' camp on Plateau Creek where arrangements were made for release of the prisoners. They were taken to the Uncompahgre Agency, where they stayed at Ouray's home on the outskirts of present Montrose. Chief Ouray and his wife Chipeta treated them with hospitality.[17]

Ralph Meeker, a son of the murdered agent, met his sister and mother here. He found them to be poorly dressed and in a highly nervous condition from their long ordeal.[18] A few days later he took them to Alamosa where they caught a train to Greeley.

In 1927 the Meeker Monument was erected three miles west of the town as a memorial to the sincere but misguided agent.

This drawing of the burned White River Agency appeared in *Frank Leslie's Illustrated Newspaper* on Dec. 6, 1879. *Photo courtesy of Denver Public Library Western Collection.*

FOOTNOTES

[1]Moffat County, C.W.A. Interviews, 1933-34, A. G. Wallihan account, pp. 136-139. In possession of the State Historical
Society of Colorado.

[2]Sidney Jocknick, *Early Days on the Western Slope of Colorado,* The Carson-Harper Co., Denver, Colo., 1913, pp. 182-183.

[3]Leroy R. and Ann W. Hafen, *Colorado,* The Old West
Publishing Co., Denver, Colo., 1949, p. 227.

[4]Marshall D. Moody, "The Meeker Massacre," *Colorado
Magazine,* April, 1953, p. 93.

[5]William N. Byers, "History of the Ute Nation," *Rocky
Mountain News,* April 16, 1880. Article in Randall Scrap
Book, pp. 13-14. In possession of the State Historical Society
of Colorado.

[6]Commissioner of Indian Affairs, *Annual Report,* 1879,
XXXII.

[7]Moody, *op. cit.,* pp. 98-99.

[8]Elizabeth Agnes Spiva, "The Utes in Colorado (1863-
1880)," 1929, p. 106, Master's Thesis, Western State College.
Manuscript in possession of Western History Department of
the Denver Public Library.

[9]Moody, *op. cit.,* p. 99.

[10]Thomas F. Dawson and F. J. V. Skiff, "The Ute War—
A History of the White River Massacre and the Privations of
the Captive White Women among the Hostiles on Grand
River," *Denver Tribune,* 1879. Articles recorded in Sidney
Jocknick, *Early Days on the Western Slope of Colorado,* Car-
son-Harper Co., Denver, Colorado, 1913, p. 192.

[11]*Ibid.,* p. 101.

[12]Records of the Bureau of Indian Affairs, Roster of Agency
Employees, 1879-80, p. 65.

[13]Rio Blanco County, C.W.A. Interviews, 1933-34, a letter

from H. A. Wildhack, April 8, 1921, p. 192. In possession of the State Historical Society of Colorado.

[14]Mansfield to Commissioner of Indian Affairs, Oct. 18, 1879. Bureau of Indian Affairs, Letters Received 1879, Colorado M. 209L.

[15]Frank Hall, *History of Colorado*, The Blakely Printing Co., Chicago, 1890, Vol. 2, pp. 503-504.

[16]*Ibid.*

[17]Contrary to the popular legend, Chipeta did not help in the rescue of the captives.

[18]Moody, *op. cit.,* p. 102.

A portrait of Major T. T. Thornburg, who was ambushed while
on his way to the aid of Meeker. Thornburg and thirteen of his
troops were killed in the initial attack. *Photo courtesy of State
Historical Society of Colorado.*

# XII

# THE AMBUSH

After Nathan Meeker, agent of the White River Agency in northwestern Colorado, sent out a plea for help to the Indian Commissioner, the War Department ordered Major T. T. Thornburg to go from Fort Steele, Wyoming Territory, to Meeker's rescue.

Thornburg marched southward from Rawlins with two companies of cavalry, two companies of infantry, and a wagon train. This amounted to a total of 140 men and thirty-three wagons.

Upon reaching Fortification Creek north of the present site of Craig, the soldiers followed the stream to where it turns westward. Here they crossed over the Flats and reached Yampa River (then called the Bear River) at its junction with Elkhead Creek, sixty-five miles north of the agency.[1]

While Thornburg was camped here, Captain Jack, ac-

compained by nine Utes, unexpectedly appeared and inquired about the purpose of the expedititon. The Indians
then learned for the first time that troops were on their
way to the White River Agency at the request of Meeker.[2]
Jack and his braves, while appearing friendly and uncon-
cerned, were greatly alarmed and distressed at this development. They left about nightfall and spread the news of
the approaching soldiers.

The next morning Thornburg continued up the Yampa to the present site of the Cary Ranch, where the troops
forded the river. They then proceeded over the hogback
to Williams Fork, arriving there on September 27th. At
this point Captain Jack and his followers again rode into
camp.

Jack proposed that Major Thornburg take an escort
of five soldiers and accompany the Indians to the agency
to talk matters over. It was evident that the Utes did not
want so many troops to come on their reservation.

Joseph Rankin, head scout of the expedition, feared
some sort of Indian trickery and advised Thornburg to re-
fuse the request.

Acting upon this advice, Thornburg told Jack that he
was going to march his men to within hailing distance of
the agency, where he would accept their proposition.[3]

Jack suggested that the troops be halted fifty miles from
the agency. Again Thornburg refused, and the ten Utes
departed.[4]

The command marched southward from Williams Fork
to Milk Creek. As the troops neared the border of the Ute
reservation twenty miles north of the present town of

Meeker, the road led through a mountain pass surrounded
on each side by high bluffs. The soldiers entered this pass
about ten o'clock on the morning of September 29, 1879.
The wagon train followed three-fourths of a mile behind.[5]

As the troops approached a much narrower defile inside the pass, Joe Rankin galloped up to Thornburg.

"That gulch just ahead would be an ideal place for an
ambush, sir. I suggest that we go around it."

Thornburg laughed at Rankin's fears, but being a good
sport, he ordered his men off the road in order to by-pass
the gully. If he had not done so, every man in his command would have been killed, for there were around 300
Ute warriors lying in wait there for the soldiers.[6]

Colorow, a ponderous, over-rated, blustering Ute; and
Antelope, a son of the great Chief Navava, who had died a
few years before, were leaders along with Captain Jack in
this ambuscade.

When the Indians saw the troops unexpectedly leave
the road to circle the arroyo, Captain Jack and Antelope
quickly reorganized their forces. Colorow, a great coward
when real danger threatened, remained too far in the background to be of any assistance.

Thornburg could see the Indians moving about, and
while incredulous of their intent to attack, he ordered his
troops back toward the wagon train three-quarters of a
mile to their rear.

The Utes started moving rapidly between the soldiers
and the train, and Rankin, an experienced Indian fighter,
advised Thornburg to open fire. The commanding officer,

however, had explicit orders from Washington not to molest the Utes in any way unless they fired on him first.

After the Utes had flanked the troops, they began shooting from both the front and rear of the retreating men.
Thornburg hastily assembled twenty cavalrymen, and riding at their head, he charged the flanking Indians in a desperate attempt to open up a hole to the wagons.

Thornburg and thirteen of his cavalry were killed in
this courageous charge, but they succeeded in driving a
wedge into the Utes' line so that the rest of the soldiers
could reach the wagon train, which was hurriedly being
formed into an irregular circle.[7] Every officer except one
had been wounded and more than 150 mules killed at the
first onslaught.

The scene of the attack was well fitted for Indian warfare. Some five hundred yards on one side of the pass a
mountain offered the attackers ample protection and enabled them to keep up a continual fire without exposing
themselves. On the other side the mountains were more
distant but still within easy rifle range.

The command was corralled on a small plateau on the
right bank of Milk Creek about one hundred yards from
the stream.[8] After Thornburg's death Captain Payne of
the Fifth Cavalry, though wounded, took charge. He set
about using the dead animals and the wagons and their
contents for breastworks. Within this ghastly enclosure
a deep circular rifle pit was dug with implements found
in the wagons. The wounded were placed inside this pit
and made as comfortable as possible.

During all this time a galling fire poured down on the

Joseph P. Rankin. *Photo courtesy State Historical Society of Colorado.*

beleaguered men from the surrounding bluffs. The cries
of the wounded and the dying could be heard above the
continual roar of the rifles. The medical officer, though
wounded himself, dressed the wounds of those most need-
ing attention.

A new danger threatened when a strong wind arose
soon after the attack was begun. Taking advantage of the
occasion, the Indians started setting fire to the dry grass
and brush to the windward of the improvised fort, hoping
to burn the defenders out. No water being at hand, the
soldiers had to smother the flames with whatever was available. After many of the wagons were badly burned, the
troops finally got the fire under control.

About four o'clock in the afternoon the savages made a
furious attack on the breastworks, but they were repulsed
and retired to the surrounding hills, where they resumed
the old tactics of picking the white men off one by one
whenever the opportunity offered.[9] The Utes believed
that starvation and thirst would in a short time so weaken
the defenders that they would be unable to resist another
charge.

During the night defenses were strengthened, and a
little water was obtained from Milk Creek by the hard-
pressed soldiers. Joseph Rankin and several other couriers
galloped off into the darkness, gambling against death
that some of them might get through the barricade of Indians and obtain help before it was too late.

For some strange reason the Ute sentinels did not see
the horsemen depart. One of the couriers had been informed that Captain F. S. Dodge and one company of

colored cavalry were on their way to the agency from Middle Park to act under the direction of Meeker in breaking up illegitimate trading and forcing a return of the Utes to their reservation. This messenger left a note on a piece of sagebrush by the side of a wagon road leading from Middle Park to Steamboat Springs which read, "Hurry up! The troops have been defeated at the agency. E.E.C."[10]

Captain Dodge found the paper on September 30th and hurried on to Hayden, which he found deserted. While he was looking through the few buildings, a group of fearful residents appeared. They had been hiding out north of town. They told Dodge what the courier had told them about the siege.

Dodge continued down the Yampa River as rapidly as possible until 4:30 P.M. when he made camp. At eight-thirty that night he repacked the wagons and sent them to a supply station on Fortification Creek with a guard of eight men.[11] He then started with the rest of his company for Milk Creek, taking with him thirty-five negro cavalrymen, four white guides, and another officer.

The night was bright and cold, and the company kept up a steady, mile-consuming jog. About four o'clock the next morning the men had ridden within five miles of their destination. A half-hour later on the third day of the siege, Dodge's cavalry reached the besieged soldiers. The Utes, apparently believing that it was a much stronger force and not wishing to expose themselves, did not fire at the newcomers until the riders were inside the wagon corral. Then, the Indians began shooting and kept it up intermittently for the next three days. Of the forty-two

Captain Jack—leader of the Thornburg ambush. *Photo courtesy of State Historical Society of Colorado.*

Chief Coloro—a participant in the Thornburg ambash. *Photo cour-tesy of Denver Public Library Western Collection.*

horses taken into the entrenchments at this time, all were killed by this gunfire except four and these were wounded.[12] While arrival of Dodge's reinforcement strengthened and encouraged Payne's beleaguered command, it was too small to change the tide of the battle.

During this siege the soldiers lived primarily on corn. Milk Creek was about one hundred yards away, and armed groups frequently ran the gauntlet of fire to secure badly needed water.

Each night the defensive works were strengthened and each day defended against renewed assaults. The greatest difficulty was in hauling out the dead animals at night and watering and feeding those that still lived.

At night some of the Indians would occasionally crawl up the creek bottom and open fire at closer range in an effort to hinder these nightly activities.

Joe Rankin, one of the couriers who escaped into the night, rode the 160 miles from Milk Creek to Rawlins, Wyoming, in twenty-eight hours.

Within a short time after Rankin reported the disastrous news, a telegram reached the garrison at Fort Russell, Wyoming Territory, which read:

> Major Thornburg is killed; Captain Payne and two other officers, including the surgeon of the command, are wounded. The command is surrounded and constantly pressed by the hostiles; fifty men are killed and wounded, and all the horses are killed.[13]

Within four hours after the telegram arrived at Fort Russell, General Wesley Merritt, one of Sheridan's most successful commanders, had all the available cavalry troops

THE BARRICADE CONSTRUCTED BETWEEN THE TWO BLUFFS OCCUPIED BY THE INDIANS.

This drawing of Thornburg's beseiged men appeared in *Frank Leslie's Illustrated Newspaper* on November 8, 1879. *Photo courtesy of Denver Public Library Western Collection.*

with their horses and equipment on a train headed for Rawlins.

By the next morning on October 2nd a force of about 200 cavalry troops and around 150 infantry troops had assembled at Rawlins. Teams and light wagons were collected in the neighborhood to carry the infantry, since the soldiers couldn't walk the 160 miles to Milk Creek in time to rescue Payne's sorely pressed command, whose provisions were sufficient to last for only three more days.

Merritt and his troops left Rawlins at 10:30 on the morning of October 2nd. They traveled forty miles that day. The second day—Friday—they made fifty miles. On Saturday they rode seventy miles, traveling day and night.

Early Sunday morning about 5:30 they unexpectedly came upon a blackened heap of ashes intermixed with fragments of iron and chains and pieces of harness. The charred wreckage proved to be George Gordon's freight outfit, loaded with a mowing machine and provisions for the agency. The freight train had been just a few miles behind Thornburg's troops at the time of the ambush. The bodies of Gordon and a fellow teamster were found farther on with distorted features and staring eyes.[14]

Upon seeting the burned ruins of Gordon's freight wagons, the guide turned to General Merritt and said. "We must be getting close. Payne can't be far from here."

Merritt brought his troops to a halt, and everyone strained his eyes and ears for a glimpse or sound of the besieged garrison or the attacking Indians. Nothing revealed the presence of either, and Merritt feared that perhaps he had arrived too late.

"It looks bad," he said to the bugler, "but go ahead and sound the Officers' Call." The Officers' Call was the night signal for the Fifth Infantry and would be recognized by any soldier of Payne's group who might still be living.

The clear notes of the trumpet broke the ominous stillness of the early dawn and eased the tension of the morning. The last notes echoed and re-echoed through the mountains and were followed by a blanketing silence. Every man in Merritt's command waited expectantly for an answering sound.

Within a few, hour-long seconds came the joyous reply of Payne's bugler, followed by the ringing cheers and glad cries of the rescued men as they rushed from their rifle pits.[15]

Merritt and his men hurried forward to greet the entrenched soldiers who had been under fire for six days.[16] Wounded men were hobbling in every direction. Nearly two hundred dead horses and mules lay within thirty feet of the breastworks filling the air with an almost intolerable stench.[17] Captain Payne hobbled forward and threw his arms around General Merritt as a child would embrace his father. Each knew it was almost a miracle that every man in Thornburg's command was not killed.

Almost simultaneously with the arrival of Merritt's troops, Sapowanero, Chief Ouray's trusted messenger, arrived with orders from the chief to cease fighting. These two events caused the rebellious Utes to give up the struggle, and they disappeared into the mountains.

The body of Major Thornburg was found stripped and mutilated where he had fallen. His remains were carried to Rawlins and shipped to Omaha, Nebraska, for burial.

After the rest of the dead were buried on the battlefield and the wounded were cared for, Captains Dodge and Payne took the remnants of their troops back to Rawlins under a strong guard. General Merritt continued on to the burned agency.

Twenty and one-half miles northeast of Meeker a monument was erected in memory of the officers, soldiers, and civilians who were killed and wounded in this battle.

As a result of this outbreak, the Northern and Uncompahgre Utes were moved out of Western Colorado. The Utes won a battle but lost an empire.

FOOTNOTES

[1] Account of A. G. Wallihan, Rio Blanco County, C.W.A. Interviews, 1933-34, Pamphlet 356, Doc. 1-73 incl., J. Monaghan interviewer, pp. 136-139. In possession of State Historical Society of Colorado.

[2] Marshall D. Moody, (Supervisor of Indian Records, National Archives, Washington, D. C.), "The Meeker Massacre," *Colorado Magazine*, April, 1953, p. 98.

[3] Thomas F. Dawson and F. J. V. Skiff, "The Ute War—a History of the White River Massacre and the Privations of the Captive White Women among the Hostiles on Grand River," *Denver Tribune*, 1879. Article recorded in Sidney Jocknick, *Early Days on the Western Slope of Colorado*, Carson-Harper Co., Denver, Colo., 1913, pp. 184-185.

[4] Moody, *op. cit.*

[5] Dawson and Skiff, *op. cit.*

[6] *Ibid.*

[7] *Ibid.* (Jocknick, p. 186).

Marker on spot of Thornburg ambush 20 miles from Meeker. *Photo courtesy of Denver Public Library Western Collection.*

[8]A letter by F. S. Dodge, Capt. Ninth Infantry, Command-
ing Co. D, at Fort Union, New Mexico, to Asst. Adj. General,
Fort Leavenworth, Missouri. Letter reproduced in Rio Blanco
Co., C.W.A. Interviews, 1933-34, pp. 60-67.

[9]General Wesley Merritt, "Three Indian Campaigns,"
*Harper's New Monthly Magazine,* 1889, reproduced in Rio
Blanco County, C.W.A. Interviews, pp. 67-70. In possession
of State Historical Society of Colorado.

[10]Dodge, *op. cit.*

[11]*Ibid.*

[12]Merritt, *op. cit.*

[13]*Ibid.*

[14]Five years later in the summer of 1884 Abram Fiske and
his son Charles, who had homesteaded land at Hayden, went
to the battleground and got the cylinder, bull wheel, and
tumbling rod of the burned mowing machine. That fall they
used these parts to assemble an improvised mowing machine
to do the little threshing that needed to be done around Hayden. That winter the Fiskes made further improvements on
the mower, and this machine did the threshing for the valley
for more than a dozen years. It was then sold to William L.
Youst of Williams Park who made use of the relic on his ranch.
Finally, in the early 1940's citizens of Hayden purchased the
historic mower and removed it to the Routt County Fair
Grounds, where it stands beside the first county court house
as a monument to pioneer days.

[15]Merritt, *op. cit.*

[16]From September 29, 1879 to October 5, 1879.

[17]Dawson and Skiff, *op. cit.,* pp. 190-191.

# XIII

# TELLURIDE'S HONEST SWINDLER

When Charles Delos Waggoner, president of the Bank of Telluride, left his office and started for home on the evening of August 29, 1929, he knew that it was only a question of time before the state bank examiners would be around to check his books and close the doors of his bank.

As he hurried up the street in his customary nervous gait, he pondered the tragic consequences of this failure to the many Telluride miners whose hard-earned savings would soon be wiped out.

In the depths of defeat, Waggoner recalled the bank's days of glory. He clearly remembered those boom years when the Bank of Telluride seemed as safe and permanent as the Rock of Gibraltar. He remembered with a wry smile how he had kept $50,000 of the bank's reserve in gold coin, which in the twenties was a symbol of security. He had frequently taken this gold from the vaults and arranged

the money in tall, neat piles in order to take pictures of it
for advertising purposes. These ads attracted customers
in the prosperous town until at one time the bank had a
deposit of $1,750,000.[1]

Then the boom days came to an end, and conditions in
Telluride went from bad to worse. He had tried to keep
the bank going through the hard times, but it had proved
to be impossible. He could not avoid the inevitable collapse which only awaited the action of the bank examiners
when they inspected the books. The only asset that the
bank had left was the confidence and trust of its depositors,
who were as yet not aware of its hopeless condition.

The small, wiry bank president acknowledged the greet-
ings of the miners who were beginning to arrive in town
after the day's work. These grimy-faced men who worked
in the gold and silver pits, these friends of his, had slaved
all their lives for the small savings they had entrusted to
him, and within only a few days at most, these hard-won
savings would be confiscated—unless he succeeded in carrying out a fantastic plan which had been gradually evolv-
ing in his worried, desperate mind during the past few days
—a gigantic, last-ditch effort which might protect the
money of the Telluride miners.

The next day on August 30th, Waggoner caught a train
for Denver to begin the execution of his plot, which was
soon to astound the entire nation. From a Western Union
office in Denver Waggoner sent a telegram in banker's code
to the First National Bank of New York. As president of
the Bank of Telluride, he had access to the various codes.

The deciphered message read, "Charge our account

for $100,000 and deposit it in the Wall Street Branch of the Chase National Bank to the credit of the Bank of Telluride." Waggoner then fraudulently signed to this communication the name of "The United States Bank of Denver."

In the same manner the Telluride banker nervously wrote telegrams in code to five other New York banks directing them to deposit specified amounts in the Chase National Bank to the account of the Bank of Telluride. To each telegram he forged the name of an affiliated Denver bank. The total amount he asked for deposit was $500,-000.

Upon receiving the telegraphic orders, all of the New York banks naively accepted the messages as authentic communications from their Denver correspondents and immediately transferred the half-million dollars to the Chase National Bank as requested.

On August 31st, a day after sending the fake telegrams from Denver, Waggoner arrived in New York and presented himself at the Central Hanover Bank where the Bank of Telluride had months previously borrowed some money. After presenting his credentials and identifying himself as president of the Bank of Telluride, he told officials of the Central Hanover Bank about the $500,000 transfer, all the time wondering if the transactions had gone through without an investigation. He was prepared for anything when one of the officials finally picked up a phone and called the Chase National Bank for certification.

"Everything appears to be in order," the official reported to Waggoner as he hung up the receiver. "The six New York banks have just finished crediting your bank with a $500,000 deposit."

So the fraudulent messages had been accepted, Waggoner thought, greatly relieved. But it was still a race with time, for as soon as the Denver banks were notified of the telegraphic orders, the crime would be discovered and all of his transactions instantly stopped.

"Well," Waggoner remarked pleasantly, trying to be casual, "since the Bank of Telluride has a little balance on hand for a change, we might as well pay up the notes we owe you."

With cashier's checks on the Bank of Telluride, Waggoner wrote out two checks to the Central Hanover Bank, one in payment of a $60,000 note and the other in payment of a $250,000 note.

Then he ordered $10,000 telegraphed to the Bank of Telluride and purchased a banker's check for the remaining $180,000. This last amount was deposited in another bank in order to scatter the stolen money around the country to prevent its recovery when the forgery came to light.

Waggoner then wrote cashier checks on this sum to pay off all other notes and obligations owed by the Telluride bank. By wiping out this indebtedness, the bank's entire resources would be available to refund its depositors when the bank was closed.

On September 3rd—just four days after the forged telegrams were sent—the astounding swindle was discovered. It was on this day that the Denver banks received word from their New York correspondents that they had com-

Charles Waggoner standing in background in Bank of Telluride. One-half million dollars in gold coin is stacked on counter. *Photo courtesy of Walker Art Studio.*

pleted the various transfers ordered in the coded telegrams. The Denver banks immediately communicated with New York and repudiated the orders as fraudulent.

Three days later on September 6th, the Bank of Telluride was closed while the state bank examiners began probing its affairs in an effort to help untangle the complicated, hopeless financial mess precipitated by the gigantic swindle.

Private, federal, and local authorities everywhere in the country began an intensive, nationwide search for the Telluride banker.

Headlines from coast to coast reported the astounding forgery. Typical of these was that in the *New York Times* which read, "A Seedy Country Banker Swindles Six New York Banks out of $500,000."

Waggoner's description appeared in most newspapers of the country: "About 5 feet 8 inches tall, 140 pounds, medium complexion, dark hair, English-cropped mustache, well dressed, somewhat nervous and jerky in his mannerisms."[2]

On September 8th private detectives hired by the American Bankers' Association turned toward Canada in the international quest for the "seedy, country banker" who had outwitted the best brains in New York.

Three days later the widespread manhunt came to an end when Waggoner was arrested at a tourist camp in Newcastle, Wyoming. News of his apprehension was flashed throughout the nation.

Waggoner realized that his capture was inevitable, and he had made no particular effort to hide. He was ready to pay the price for his actions, which he believed were justified to protect the depositors of his bank.

"I knew exactly what I was doing," he confessed to authorities. "There is no one to blame but myself. I was the one who sent the fake telegrams out of Denver to the six New York banks, and neither my wife, my family, nor any of the Telluride bank officials had anything to do with the affair. The bottom had dropped out of things in Telluride, and a desperate move was necessary. I would rather see the New York banks lose money than the people of Telluride, most of whom had worked all their lives for the savings which were deposited in my bank."[3]

"Are you sure that all this financial muddle you've caused will protect your depositors?" an officer asked dubiously.

"Definitely," Waggoner replied. "The money involved is so widely scattered throughout the country that it can never be retrieved. The debts of my bank have been paid with that money, and since I alone am guilty of any wrong doing, the Bank of Telluride cannot be forced to make good the loss. Only I can be punished. It is the 'perfect crime'."

Waggoner was put under $100,000 bond and transferred from Newcastle to Cheyenne in irons. He was then taken to New York to stand trial.

In closing his case at the widely publicized trial, Defense Attorney Alan R. Campbell said, "Charles Delos Waggoner is a Robin Hood who stole from the rich to protect poor depositors. He did not profit personally from the deal but used all the money for payment of claims against the Telluride Bank."[4]

The defendant was sentenced to fifteen years in the federal penitentiary at Atlanta, Georgia. After serving six years of his sentence, Waggoner was paroled in May, 1935. His wife, who had remained steadfastly loyal throughout the long ordeal, was there to greet him when he walked out of the prison gates.

The next few years were lean ones for the paroled prisoner. The glamor of his crime had worn off, and he was no longer considered a Robin Hood who had robbed the rich to give to the poor. He was just another ex-con trying futilely to find a suitable job. When his efforts to find employment failed, for a short time he tried operating a little bakery in Georgia.[5] However, this was out of his line and did not prove successful.

Finally, during the summer of 1937, Waggoner wrote a letter to an old Telluride acquaintance, J. Walter Eames, asking for employment. Eames had moved from Telluride to Grand Junction, where he operated the Biltmore Club.[6]

The story is told that years before when both men were living in Telluride, Eames was at one time badly in need of money. Waggoner helped him out to the extent of $500, which put Eames back on his feet.[7] When Eames received Waggoner's request many years later, he repaid the debt by giving his former benefactor a job—the one man who befriended the honest bank swindler.[8]

FOOTNOTES

[1]*The Daily Sentinel,* Feb. 15, 1939, p. 1.

[2]Description of Waggoner obtained from interviews with Dick Raber, Mel Springer, and M. H. Crissman—fellow Western Slope bankers who were acquainted with him.

[3]*The Daily Sentinel,* Feb. 15, 1939, p. 1.

[4]*Ibid.*

[5]*Rocky Mountain News,* Feb. 15, 1939.

[6]*Ibid.*

[7]*The Daily Sentinel,* Feb. 15, 1939.

[8]On December 18, 1939, three masked gunmen while attempting to hold up the Biltmore Club shot down and killed Walter Eames.

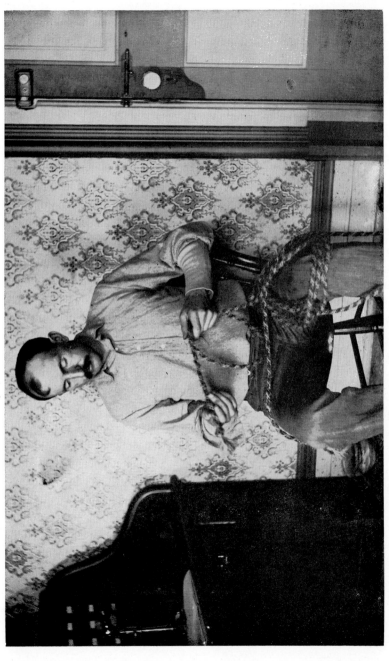

Tom Horn in office of Cheyenne jail shortly before he was hanged. *Photo courtesy of Wyoming State Historical Department, Wagner Collection*

# XIV

# PROFESSIONAL KILLER

Brown's Park, an almost level valley thirty miles long and five miles wide, lying along the Green River in north-western Colorado, was in the 1830's and 1840's a famous rendezvous site for mountain men and fur trappers. Later on after cattle ranches were established there, it became notorious as a hideout for outlaws. Toward the turn of the century it also was the scene of a bitter struggle between the big and small cattle owners.

In the 80's and early 90's Brown's Park was a favorite winter grazing land for the big cattle outfits in north-western Colorado, which the cattle kings ruled without competition. Then, during the latter part of the 90's the small cattlemen in the area began to get into the way of the cattle barons. It was not an uncommon practice in those early days for the little operators to put their brands on mavericks from the large ranches. In Brown's Park

cattle started disappearing from the big herds at an alarm-
ing rate while some of the small ones began expanding
amazingly fast.

There was so much cattle rustling going on in the park
that whenever two men met on the range they would ride
around one another like two strange bull dogs.  If one of
them waved his hat directing the other to ride around so
that they could not identify each other, the request was
nearly always complied with.  Cowboys and cattlemen were
as alert and wary as coyotes.  They kept out of sight as much
as possible, riding up and down ravines and gulches while
continually looking for tracks.  If they had to venture
through an open stretch, they usually first rode up on the
summit of some hill to examine the country below for possible signs of human life.[1]

Ora Haley, owner of the famous Two-bar outfit, was
the largest cattle rancher in northwestern Colorado at this
time.  When he learned that his cattle were being stolen, he
asked Hi Bernard, his foreman, what should be done to
remedy the situation.

"Lease a bunch of cattle to Charlie Ayers," Bernard
advised.  "He's experienced in such matters.  If the rustlers
start working on him, he will know who he can get to stop
them."[2]

Haley followed his foreman's advice, and in the fall of
1900 the widely known rustler exterminator, Tom Horn,
rode down into Brown's Park from Wyoming.  No one
knows definitely for whom he was working, but in a later
confession Horn said that his usual price was $600 for
every cattle thief he killed or forced to leave the country.[3]

Tom Horn was an enigmatical character, combining both the best and the worst qualities of the early-day frontiersman. He helped bring law and order to the west, but could not adjust himself to the new order which he had helped establish. In his checkered career he had helped track down train robbers, acted as an army scout, served as a colonel in the Spanish-American war, worked on numerous cattle ranches, and in 1888 at Phoenix he became nationally known by breaking the world's record for steer roping and tying.[4]

He was an imposing figure of a man. He stood six feet two inches tall, was arrow straight, deep chested, and lean loined. He was a first class cowpuncher, crack shot, deadly trailer, and a courageous soldier.

Yet, in spite of all these admirable traits, there was a kink in his character. While loyal and generous toward those in his camp, he placed no value on the life of an antagonist. If possible, he would shoot his victims from ambush without giving them a chance. This cruel and treacherous side to his nature was evidenced only by his shifting eyes, which never looked at a person directly.

Afer arriving at Brown's Park, Horn worked for various cattle outfits in order to familiarize himself with the rustling situation.

Among the people he worked for was Mat Rash. Rash had come from Texas as a cowboy, settled in Brown's Park, and built up a small herd of cattle, which was increasing at a rapid rate. Horn soon found out the reason for this growth and put Rash down on his list.[5]

Horn also learned about Isam Dart—a colored man—

who had frequently been in trouble with the law and who once had escaped from the sheriff while awaiting trial at Hahn's Peak for stealing livestock.[6] Horn discovered that Isam had not mended his ways and had, furthermore, taken up some strategic waterholes which were interfering with the interests of the big cowmen.[7]

Horn also became very much interested in E. B. "Longhorn" Thompson's various activities. Longhorn had a ranch that joined the Two-bar on the Little Snake River. Often after the fall roundups the strays would be put into Longhorn's pasture, and he was supposed to notify the various owners. Longhorn would notify the owners, but when they arrived to take home the branded strays and dispose of the unbranded animals, Thompson's fence was usually found down and the cattle gone.[8] It was remarkable how few of the "slick" strays were ever seen again without Longhorn's brand on them.

Early that summer Isam Dart, Mat Rash, and Longhorn Thompson each received a note from Horn ordering them to leave Brown's Park in thirty days or take the consequences. He signed these warnings with his usual alias "Tom Hicks," a name which was widely known and feared by cattle rustlers.

One evening after the thirty days had expired, Tom Horn rode up to Mat Rash's cabin and dismounted. Mat had butchered a calf and was frying a steak for supper when Horn appeared at the open door.

"Hello there, Horn," Mat greeted. "You're just in time for supper. Come on in and I'll cut off another steak."

"Mat," Horn said, drawing his six-shooter, "I have come to kill you."

"What's this all about?" Mat asked in bewilderment, glancing at his revolver and scabbard lying just out of reach on the bed.

"I'm Tom Hicks," Horn explained, shooting as he spoke.

Mat fell to the floor, and Horn shot him again. Then Horn jumped on his horse and galloped away. The wounded man crawled to his bunk. With a last effort he pulled a pencil and paper from his pocket but died before he was able to write down his message.[9]

When Isam Dart heard about Mat's death, he knew that "Tom Hicks" had arrived to keep his promise. He had heard of the notorious killer before, but, like Mat Rash, did not know who he was. Fearful that he was next on "Hicks' " list, the negro was afraid to venture out of his cabin for several days. Finally, early one morning he found the courage to hasten out of the cabin toward his pasture. He intended to catch a horse and beat a hasty retreat out of Brown's Park.

Tom Horn was hiding behind a tree near the corral patiently awaiting him. When Isam was about sixty yards distant, Horn jerked up his Manchester rifle and fired. The slug grazed Isam's heart as it passed through his body. The stricken man leaped high into the air and fell to the ground—dead. Horn put rocks under the dead man's head in conformance with his usual custom so as to prove to his employers that he was the killer. These rocks were his trademark. Then he ran down into the gulch where his horse was tied and rode in the direction of Longhorn Thompson's ranch.

One evening not long afterwards Longhorn was riding along the Little Snake River toward his home when he saw the figure of a man raise up over the brush with a Manchester in his hands. Terrified, Thompson spurred his horse into the willows and raced out of gun range.

Knowing that his life was in serious jeopardy, Thompson abandoned his ranch and moved to Craig. Fearful of what his pursuer might do, he kept his shades down and his lamps out. One night as he was returning home, he spied the shadowy figure of a man hiding behind a tree near his yard. Believing the man to be the legendary Tom Hicks, Thompson pulled up stakes at Craig and went into hiding at Vernal, Utah.

For some reason or other Horn did not try to kill Thompson, for he could have easily done so. Apparently he just wanted to scare the rustler out of the country. Nevertheless, Thompson boasted that he was the only man that Tom Hicks ever went after and failed to get.

One day in Denver more than a year later, a stranger stepped up to Horn and said, "Ain't your name Hicks or Horn?"

"What is it to you?" Horn asked suspiciously.

"Why, I'm from Montana, and my name is Sparks. We're lookin' for a man like you to do a job for us. The gray wolves is gettin' our cattle, and we don't know whether they're four-legged or two."

"That's my business," Horn said, his suspicions fading.

"I'll take your offer. That is, if I can git a down payment.
I'm a little short of cash."

"I'll have to go to Cheyenne to get the money, Horn.
I'll meet you there, say in three nights from now if you can
make it."

After making detailed arrangements as to the time and
place of their proposed meeting, the two men parted company.[10]

Three nights later on January 12, 1902, they met again
in a room of a Cheyenne hotel. Before getting down to the
business at hand, Horn's companion gave him quite a number of strong drinks. Horn was a heavy drinker and accepted them without realizing it was all part of a trap to
make him talk.

"What about my security?" Horn finally brought up
the subject that he had come to discuss.

"Me and my associates are willin' to advance you some
money," the quiet-voiced stranger answered, "but first
we'd like to know something about what you've done so
that we can be sure you can handle the work."

After all of his drinks Horn was in a talkative mood.
Believing that a job was at stake, he told about some of the
rustlers he had killed or run out of the country for $600 a
head.

"Ain't you the one who killed that fourteen-year-old
Wyoming boy—Willie Nickell. You know, Kels Nickell's
kid?"

Horn hesitated before answering. "Yes, I shot him, but
that's one killing I regret. I was layin' in wait for Kels
when his boy came out the gate on some errand or other

and saw me hiding there behind a rock. I had to shoot the kid to keep him from running back to the house and raising a big commotiton."[11]

As soon as Horn had finished speaking, the door to an adjoining room suddenly opened, and the sheriff sprang in and covered Horn with his guns. He and a stenographer had been hidden in the next room listening and taking notes on everything that Horn had said. Horn's would-be employer proved to be Joe La Fors, a deputy United States marshal.

Tom looked at the marshal and said, "By God, it won't be long before you'll be sleepin' on a pile of my rocks."

Tom had many staunch friends among the big cattle ranchers who pooled their funds to hire the best defense lawyer available. Horn's defense was based primarily on the grounds that he had been framed by the sheriff and the marshal and they had made up his alleged confession to Marshal La Fors. The preponderance of evidence, however, was against him, and the jury convicted him of the murder of Willie Nickell and sentenced him to die.

A short time before the execution, state guards were called out to help prevent the prisoner from being rescued. Until the last, Horn believed that the cattlemen who had hired him would either bring about a commutation of sentence or help him escape.

A day or so before he walked to his death, he was offered a promise of freedom if he would turn state's evidence and name the men who had put up the money for his killings. But he refused.[12]

On November 20, 1903, the day that he was hanged,

300 soldiers were on hand to keep order. From his cot in the jail Horn could hear the huge crowd milling around. It was only ten minutes before the time set for execution, and Horn calmly puffed on a cigar as he lay on his cot writing a farewell letter to his friend John C. Coble in which he stated that his alleged confession had been composed by the officers even before he came to Cheyenne. He concluded, "This is the truth as I am going to die in ten minutes."[13]

When he was escorted up on the ten foot scaffold, he nodded a friendly greeting to his many cowboy friends who spoke encouragingly to him from the crowd.

"Don't worry, Tom," one of them shouted. "A posse of your friends will be here right away to get you down."

Horn helped the undersheriff and his assistant adjust the straps and noose. He smiled as the hood was slipped over his head.

County Clerk Joseph Cahill took Horn's arm to help him mount the trapdoors. A two-and-one-half gallon bucket of water acted as the trap trigger. When sufficient water leaked out of the bucket, the doors would be sprung, leaving the condemned man dangling at the end of a four foot slack of rope.

Feeling the clerk's hand trembling as the two men approached the trapdoors, Tom Horn uttered his last words, "Ain't losin' your nerve, are you, Joe?"[14]

FOOTNOTES

[1]Moffat County, C.W.A. Interviews, 1933-34, Account of Carey Barber, pp. 215-219. In possession of State Historical Society of Colorado.

[2]*Ibid.,* Account of E. V. Houghy, pp. 140-143.

[3]Charles H. Leckenby, "Tom Horn was a Killer," *The Tread of Pioneers,* The Steamboat Pilot Press, Steamboat Springs, Colorado, 1945, pp. 157-160.

[4]William MacLeod Raine, "The Enigma of Tom Horn," *Empire Magazine,* Feb. 8, 1953.

[5]Routt and Arapaho Counties, C.W.A. Interviews, 1933-34, "Echoes of a Pioneer Cowman," pp. 158-160.

[6]Leckenby, *op. cit.*

[7]Moffat County, *op. cit.,* Tom Blevin's Account of Tom Horn, pp. 144-148.

[8]Moffat County, *op. cit.,* E. V. Houghy Account, pp. 140-143.

[9]Routt and Arapaho Counties, *op. cit.,* pp. 158-160.

[10]Moffat County, *op. cit.,* E. V. Houghy Account, pp. 140-143.

[11]Leckenby, *op. cit.*

[12]Moffat County, *op. cit.,* E. V. Houghy Account, pp. 140-143.

[13]Leckenby, *op. cit.*

[14]*Ibid.*

## XV

# THE DOUBLE-CROSS[1]

During the late summer of 1865 Joseph Hahn, William Doyle, and Captain George Way journeyed over Berthoud Pass and through Middle and North Parks to the foot of what is now known as Hahns Peak in the northern part of Routt County, Colorado. Here on Willow Creek Joseph Hahn had discovered traces of gold three years before.

The three prospectors found patches of gold-bearing sand and gravel on all sides of the towering peak but not in sufficient quantities to pay for work with the pan, which was their only means of washing it. However, their findings caused them to believe that sooner or later they would make a strike. It being too late in the season to continue their search before winter closed in, they decided to return the following summer as soon as the weather permitted.

Before making the long trek back to civilization on the eastern side of the Continental Divide, William Doyle and George Way climbed the great peak, leaving their older partner—Joseph Hahn—in camp. Upon finally reaching the summit, Doyle pulled from a pocket an empty waterproof Preston and Merrill baking powder can with a screw top. In this can he placed a sheet of paper on which he had scribbled, "This is named Hahns Peak by his friend and comrade William A. Doyle, August 27, 1865."

After the three associates arrived on the Eastern Slope, they separated for the winter. But on July, 1866, they and about fifty other hopeful prospectors gathered together at the town of Empire near the foot of Berthoud Pass to renew explorations in the Hahns Peak region.

This group of men was a typical cross section of the early day prospectors of Colorado. They represented nearly every section of the United States and almost every country of the world. Long whiskers concealed youthful faces, and few, if any, showed signs of graying hair. Colorado's pioneer prospectors were young men. They had to be to withstand the exposures, privations, and hardships which went with prospecting for gold in the uncharted wilderness.

They were roughly clad in the usual prospector's garb of shirts, trousers, and boots appropriate to heavy work. Sleds and pack animals were piled high with the customary prospecting provisions and equipment—shovels, pans, and axes, frying pans, coffee pots, tin cups, tin plates, butcher knives, and iron spoons, flour, sugar, salt, bacon, beans, and coffee, and clothing, blankets, and buffalo robes.

Although it was mid-summer the party ran into a big blizzard on Berthoud Pass and had to shovel out a trail through the deep, soft snow for their sleds and pack animals. While lying in their blankets one night at the present site of Hot Sulphur Springs, one of the prospectors poetically remarked, "The sweetest of all rest is on the bosom of old mother earth, watched by the sentinel stars, and lulled by the sad-hearted pine and falling water."

As the explorers made their way through Middle and North Parks, they kept their weapons handy, for they were in Ute Indian country. Fortunately, however, no Indians happened to see the intruders.

Crossing the Big Muddy above Hilt Creek a number of miles north of the present town of Kremmling, Joseph Hahn led his party over the Rabbit Ears Range through a pass which he had discovered in 1862. Finally on August 27, 1866—after more than a month enroute—the prospectors reached their destination in the shadows of Hahns Peak.

Some commenced building cabins while others began looking for gold. Many of the main gulches which the discoverers worked were named after members of the expedition and the various countries and states from which they hailed. Some of the names have continued to this day, including Hahn's Gulch, German Gulch, Doyle's Gulch, Nova Scotia Gulch, Way's Gulch, and Virginia Gulch.

William Doyle—one of the three original partners—was the first to hit pay dirt. One day while prospecting in a little ravine, he took out a pan that contained gold dust worth from five to ten dollars. This discovery convinced the optimistic group that they all would soon strike it rich. So, to protect their claims, they organized a mining district and drew up laws patterned after those of the Central City district. An election was then held to choose a sheriff, judge, surveyor, recorder, and a board of commissioners. Among those elected were Joseph Hahn, surveyor; William Doyle, recorder; and George Way, judge.

Before the miners loaded on their packs and started for the Eastern Slope on October 1st to escape the fast approaching cold winter, they had panned a considerable amount of gold. Most of them had staked out valuable claims which they intended to come back to the following spring.

The three partners—Joseph Hahn, Captain George Way, and William Doyle—did not leave with the others. They decided to spend the winter at Hahns Peak in order to make preparations for early washing in the spring on the rich bars that they had discovered. To remain, however, it was necessary to replenish their fading supply of food. So, on October 2nd Captain George Way set out for Empire, taking with him all of the gold dust that the three had found to pay for the provisions which he planned to return with.

"I'll be back by October 14th," he remarked.

"You can't make the round-trip that soon, Cap," Hahn answered in his strong German accent, "but if you get back by the 20th, all will be well."

While awaiting the return of their comrade, Hahn and Doyle worked hard. They built a cabin and whipsawed lumber to be used in their work the following season.

When the captain had not shown up by November 1st, Hahn and Doyle shot some game to replenish their depleted food supply. They did not waste too much time hunting, believing that their partner would make his appearance at any hour.

November 24th rolled around, and still Captain Way had not arrived. By this time the ground was covered with several feet of snow, and game was hard to find. It snowed every day from November 24th to December 31st, piling up the snow to twelve feet on the level. Rabbits were now the only edible animals remaining in the region, and they were not plentiful.

Doyle and Hahn managed to survive on a meager diet of rabbit until April, still trusting that Way would come to their rescue. By the last of April they finally gave up hope, believing that some accident must have befallen their comrade. They never suspected that their trusted friend had absconded with the gold, leaving them to their tragic fate.[2]

Both men were gaunt and weak from months of exposure and improper diet. In spite of their feeble condition, they packed a few belongings and on April 22, 1866, started on snowshoes for Empire—more than a hundred miles away. They had waited too long, and both knew that they would probably die on the way.

A week later on April 29th the ill-fated prospectors, worn out and snow-blinded, paused to get their wind on the banks of the Big Muddy in Middle Park.

After a time Doyle struggled to his feet, "Let's get goin', Joe. We can still make another mile or two before dark."

"I'm done for, Bill," Hahn answered, making no effort to rise. "I can't go no further."

"Oh, you're not licked yet, Joe," Doyle said, trying to hide his uneasiness. "We'll make camp here for the night, and by tomorrow you'll be rarin' to go."

Doyle spread out their blankets and made his companion as comfortable as possible. He then found some dry wood, lighted a fire, and cooked the last remnants of a jack rabbit that he had shot the day before. Hahn was running a high fever and was not hungry. However, Doyle insisted that he take a few bites to keep up his waning strength.

When it was dark, Doyle lay down beside Hahn. During the night Hahn became delirious and began mumbling incoherently in his native tongue. The next morning Doyle tried to get his sick friend to eat the rest of the rabbit that he had cooked on the previous evening, but Hahn was too far gone to eat anything.

In one of his rare moments of rationality, he said, "For God's sake, Bill, get goin' and try to save yourself."

"Don't give up, Joe," Doyle answered. "I'm going to look for help."

When he returned that night after futilely wandering around looking for a sign of human life, Hahn was lying dead between the blankets. Too weak to bury his comrade, Doyle continued on his seemingly hopeless journey. He crossed the Big Muddy and made his way to the Troublesome. Here he was miraculously found, snowblinded and exhausted, by three trappers who were spending the winter in this locality. Doyle remained with them until he had regained his strength before continuing on to Empire.

Hahn's skeleton was discovered on the banks of the Big Muddy during the summer by a fisherman, who was able to identify the remains by certain papers which he found in Hahn's wallet. Paul Lindstrom, a relative of the dead man, was duly notified. That November Lindstrom sent Jack Sumner to bury Hahn. William N. Byers, the founder of Hot Sulphur Springs, assisted in the burial.

The grave was marked by a pile of rocks, and a broken snowshoe was placed at its head. There was no epitaph on the snowshoe, but if there had been one, it could have read, "Joseph Hahn, a pioneer of northwestern Colorado, lies buried here because he was double-crossed by a trusted friend."

FOOTNOTES

[1]Charles H. Leckenby, "Discovery of Gold at Hahns Peak and the Tragic Death of Joseph Hahn," *The Steamboat Pilot Press,* Steamboat Springs, Colo., 1945.

[2]Way lived in Colorado for many years after this event. He finally died at Georgetown, New Mexico, in 1883.

## XVI

# THE DIAMOND PEAK STORY

Colorado is a state of high peaks. Of these, Diamond Peak, which stands in the extreme northwestern corner of the state near the Wyoming border, is unique, for it was named in memory of a story—a story about a diamond field.

In 1872 when this unusual and nearly forgotten drama took place, Professor Henry Janin was the most eminent geologist in the United States. During that summer he was hired by a syndicate of San Francisco bankers to go on what proved to be the most fateful mission of his long and illustrious career.

All during the spring and early summer of 1872 fantastic reports had been circulating throughout the nation about the discovery of a fabulous gem mine somewhere in the Wyoming and Colorado Territories. The instigator of these rumors was Philip Arnold, a prospector

from Kentucky.[1] He told newspaper reporters that he
and his partner, Captain Slack, an old California miner,
had found a claim containing great wealth in diamonds,
rubies, emeralds, sapphires, and garnets. While he would
not give the exact location of the field, he said that he
and Slack had been guided to the place by an Indian.[2]

In promoting the project before a group of San Francisco bankers, Arnold produced a small sack filled with
rough precious stones as representative of the gems that
he had found on the property. After a well-known jeweler
verified the genuineness of the raw stones, the San Francisco syndicate became seriously interested in the alleged
discovery.

The bankers hoped that this new strike would replace
the very valuable Comstock Lode of Virginia City, Nevada,
in which they had an interest. The Comstock Lode, one of
the largest silver mines ever to be discovered, was on the
down grade, and the syndicate welcomed an opportunity
to find something of comparative value to take its place.

Accordingly, the bankers agreed to purchase the diamond field for a huge sum provided that Arnold and Slack
could prove the value of their claim to the renowned geologist, Professor Henry Janin.[3]

Janin accompanied the partners to the diamond field
to make the investigation. They traveled by train as far
as Rawlins, Wyoming Territory, and then proceeded south
across the Red Desert on horseback, carrying their provisions and equipment on a pack horse. Before reaching
their destination, Janin was blindfolded to prevent him
from learning the exact location of the claim.

A few miles north of what is now known as Diamond
Peak, Arnold removed the blindfold and told the professor that he was now in the vicinity of the diamond field.

For several days Janin scraped around the region, un-
covering raw diamonds, rubies, sapphires, emeralds, and
garnets, all of which he immediately recognized to be gen-
uine.

"I can hardly believe my eyes," the excited geologist
commented to his two companions. "This field will make
the mines in South Africa look like thirty cents."

After collecting a quantity of the precious stones, the
three men hastened back to San Francisco, where Janin
made a full report of his investigation. In this account he
verified the representations of Arnold and Slack.

Janin's favorable report was reproduced in newspapers
all over the country, causing profound national interest in
the great discovery. On the basis of Janin's observations,
the San Francisco syndicate purchased the claim for several million dollars and prepared to start operations as
quickly as possible.[4]

In the meantime, Clarence King, another well-known
geologist, read Janin's report. He recognized the region
described as one which he himself had recently surveyed.
Knowing that it would be a blot upon his survey not to
have found some evidence of this immense diamond field,
he decided to make another examination.[5]

King reached the diamond claim on November 2, 1872,
and made a thorough investigation. Like Janin he found
a number of precious gems, but among the raw stones, he

also discovered a few partially cut and partially polished stones.

This evidence confirmed King's suspicions that Arnold and Slack had sowed the alleged diamond field. Apparently they had purchased the raw gems from some precious stone broker, who had unintentionally got a few partly worked stones in with the rough ones. Failing to notice this discrepancy, the swindlers had planted the partially cut and polished stones along with the raw gems.

King hurried to San Francisco to expose the fraud. The startled bankers sent out another expedition, which was accompanied by both Janin and King. This investigation proved beyond a doubt that the claim had been salted.

The swindle received international attention. Upon reading the headlines in a London newspaper, a broker in precious stones wrote to the San Francisco syndicate that two Americans answering the description of Arnold and Slack had come to his office several times during the winter and spring of 1872. They had shown him a letter of credit for a considerable amount of money and had purchased rough diamonds and gems of all kinds and descriptions.[6]

Arnold and Slack admitted that they had bought the stones abroad and paid duty on them into Canada. From there they smuggled the gems into the United States so that there would be no record of their being brought into the country.

In spite of their misrepresentation, Arnold and Slack were never prosecuted. In those early years mining laws were so undeveloped that misrepresenting and selling a claim was apparently in the same category as misrepresent-

---

ing and selling a horse.[7] If you got stung, it was just your hard luck.

The person most hurt by the swindle was Henry Janin. Since he had endorsed the project, his reputation in this country as a geologist was ruined. Consequently, the professor left the United States and started a new career in England. With his remarkable ability, it did not take him long to once more gain recognition as one of the greatest geologists of his time. A protege of Janin's was a young mining engineer named Herbert Hoover, who examined mineral resources for the geologist in China, Burma, and South Africa.

Even up to recent times, people have scoured the area of the mythical mine in search of any hidden treasure which might have remained undiscovered throughout the years.

While today all of the treasure and many of the facts concerning the spectacular swindle have been lost in the mists of time, Diamond Peak stands as a perpetual memory to a fantastic legend which will never completely be forgotten.

FOOTNOTES

[1]Kenneth Hickok (former professor at the Colorado School of Mines), personal interview, Oct. 1955.

[2]Charles H. Leckenby, "A Diamond Swindle," *The Tread of Pioneers*, The Steamboat Pilot Press, Steamboat Springs, Colo., 1945.

[3]Hickock, *op. cit.*

[4]*Ibid.*
[5]Leckenby, *op. cit.*
[6]Leckenby, *op. cit.*
[7]Hickock, *op. cit.*

## XVII

# THE PRICE OF HAY

On the evening of August 4, 1890, eight men sat visiting in a cabin on the East Muddy about forty miles northeast of the nine-year-old town of Paonia, Colorado. The cabin belonged to Johnny McNaughton, Jim Bainard, and Ed Harbinson, partners in the ownership of a small cattle ranch. The other five men were newcomers from Kansas, and they were staying at the cabin until they could get located in the region.[1]

The Kansas group had spent the day clearing rocks, brush, and logs off a twenty-acre mountain park situated nearly three miles southeast of the cabin. They intended to start cutting and putting up the hay on the following day to get their few head of stock through the winter.

The conversation was interrupted by a loud knock on the door. Ed Harbinson opened the door where he was confronted by an irate Irishman by the name of Thomas

Welch. Welch was prospecting for placer mines in the Muddy country, and he had built a cabin some years before about three miles southeast of the park where the five Kansas men had been working.[2]

"It looks like you was making preparations to cut hay on my meadow," he said belligerently.

"Now, listen here, Tom," Harbinson replied, "that park is government land, and we have just as much right to that wild hay as you have."

"If you cut hay on that meadow," Welch warned, "it will be over my dead body."[3]

Without more ado Welch strode over to his horse, mounted, and rode away.

"What's he so excited about?" Alexander Labelle commented as Harbinson closed the door.

"Just because he's cut hay on that park for his burros during the last two or three years, he thinks the place belongs to him."

There were a few flippant remarks about the Irishman's hot-headedness, and then the subject was changed. No one took Welch's threat seriously, believing that at worst a free-for-all fist fight would settle ownership of this fall's cutting.

The next afternoon about two o'clock[4] when the hay crew was ready to start out, Harbinson decided at the last minute to accompany his Kansas friends in order to see the fight which everyone expected to ensue. As a precautionary measure in case things got too rough, he brought along his .45-.90 caliber rifle. He jumped up on the wagon beside the mowing machine which was being hauled to the disputed field. Charles Major, the driver, clucked to the team, and the party was on its way. Riding behind the wagon were H. D. Jones, Alexander Labelle, Charles Purham, and Peter Small, none of whom was carrying a gun.[5] Jim Bainard and Johnny McNaughton remained at the cabin.

When the park finally came into view, no one was in sight, and everything appeared serene and peaceful. In the distance the men could see the tall grass swaying gently in the mountain breeze, resembling gentle waves on a small sea.

"Nice lookin' crop," Charles Purham remarked.

"Well, Ed," Alexander Labelle said above the rumbling of the wagon, "yuh might as well lay down your rifle. I don't see any sign of our Irish friend."

"It's funny," Charles Major remarked. "From the way he talked last evening, I sure thought he meant business."

The visiting was terminated as the wagon rattled on to the grassy clearing. Each man felt a strange tenseness—a premonition of danger that he could not define. The fragrant wild hay brushed against the horses' bellies as they were guided through the luxurious growth.

"Take a look at that old log over there about forty feet," Peter Small said, interrupting the ominous silence. "I don't remember seein' them rocks chucked around it when we was here yesterday."

All eyes turned toward the gigantic spruce log, which they had left in the northwest corner of the field because of its great weight.

"It looks like someone has tried to plug up the dips

underneath all right," Alexander Labelle agreed. "It would make a good barricade."

He had hardly finished speaking when the muzzle of a rifle appeared over the log, and a shot boomed through the mountains. The bullet spat against the mower and whirred loudly off into space.

"Run for cover," Harbinson yelled.

As if the shot were a signal, the entire East Muddy was instantly echoing and reechoing with gun reports. Charles Purham, Alexander Labelle, and Peter Small were knocked from their horses seriously wounded. H. D. Jones rolled unhurt off his mount into the high grass and hugged the ground. The terrified, riderless horses stampeded across the park and disappeared in the surrounding forest of spruce and aspen.

At the first onslaught Charles Major and Ed Harbinson leaped from the wagon. Major lay down behind a wagon wheel, still holding the reins. He kept speaking to the gentle team in order to keep them from running away. Harbinson dropped down in a little sink, holding his rifle in readiness.[6]

Bullets smashed against the wagon and beat a terrifying tatoo on the iron wheels of the mowing machine. Arthur Wade, who was riding horseback several miles away, heard the shooting and decided that a group of hunters had run on to a large herd of deer or elk.

While crouched in the grass, Harbinson observed that the barricaded spruce log hid the killer who was doing most of the shooting. Quickly raising his rifle, Harbinson returned the fire. When the bullet hit the rocks just under the log, the top of an old dilapidated hat arose just above the bulwark. Quickly reloading, Harbinson took speedy aim at the barely visible hat band. He jerked on the trigger, and the hat vanished from view.

The resounding reports suddenly ceased and a menacing quiet followed. It was unexpectedly broken by Thomas Welch's hoarse voice, which bawled out from the encircling timber, "Take your dead and get the hell out of here!"

Charles Major, Ed Harbinson, and H. D. Jones hesitantly raised themselves above the grass—the lone survivors of the ambush.

Alexander Labelle was dead. Peter Small lay mortally wounded and died the next day. He and Alexander Labelle were buried behind Ed Harbinson's cabin, where they still lie. Charles Purham was found in a serious condition and died a year or so later from after-effects of his injury.

After Charles Major and Ed Harbinson had driven away with their dead and wounded, Thomas Welch, Ed "Butcherknife" Hardesty, Schuyler Hoddson, George Dufford, Nick Anderson, and Welch's younger son, Robert, came out of the trees where they had been hiding. There beside the decaying log they found the body of sixteen-year-old Thomas Welch, Jr., with a bullet through his head. He was put on a pack horse, and his father took him to Carbondale for burial.

A day or so after the battle, Arthur Wade and Lillie Mae Stephens, Wade's future wife, visited the scene of the ambush. There behind the big log Lillie found a piece of the dead boy's skull with some of his red hair still attached.[7]

A line was surveyed to determine whether the gun battle took place in Delta County or Gunnison County. After the survey showed that it occured in Gunnison County, charges were brought by the district attorney against all participating parties.

Thomas Welch was arrested by Garfield County authorities and brought to Gunnison. Ed Hardesty and Schuyler Hoddson of the Welch party were captured in Montrose County. All other members of both sides came to Gunnison voluntarily to appear before the grand jury, which was investigating the case.[8]

The jury indicted Thomas Welch, Ed Hardesty, and Schuyler Hoddson. The other two members of the Welch group—George Dufford and Nick Anderson—were not indicted because they produced satisfactory evidence that they did not do any of the shooting. Harbinson and his crew were not brought to trial because it was shown that Harbinson shot Thomas Welch, Jr., in self-defense.[9]

After a lengthy trial Welch and his two associates were acquitted in April, 1891,[10] on the grounds that the dead boy did the actual killing of Labelle and Purham.

Everything considered, Tom Welch paid a high price for his fall hay cutting.

FOOTNOTES

[1]Parker Balch, personal interview, 1955.
[2]*Gunnison Review Press*, Aug. 30, 1890.

[3]Arthur Wade, personal interview, 1936.
[4]*Gunnison Tribune,* April 4, 1891.
[5]Wade, *op. cit.*
[6]*Ibid.*
[7]*Ibid.*
[8]*Gunnison Review Press,* Aug. 16, 1890.
[9]*Ibid.*
[10]*Gunnison Tribune,* April 18, 1891.

## XVIII

# A RACE FOR JUSTICE

In the semi-arid west, where the value of a ranch or the growth of a town is dependent largely on the amount of its available water, westerners have fought over this precious life-blood ever since the area was opened for settlement. In western Colorado an early illustration of this age-old struggle occurred July 2, 1890, on California Mesa just over the Montrose County line between Delta and Olathe, Colorado.

In the late 1880's Mark Powers and his sister took up a homestead on California Mesa. The elderly newcomers were quiet, unsociable, and industrious. They cleared their land, built fences, and dug irrigation ditches.[1]

One Sunday morning on July 2, 1890,[2] Powers and his sister noticed a man at their headgate. Picking up his rifle, Powers walked up to where the man was diverting water from Powers' ditch down the main canal.[3] He proved to be Charles Bear, another resident of California Mesa who had a ranch a short distance below.

"You leave my water alone!" Powers said belligerently.

"You're takin' more than your share, Powers," Bear said. "If you keep this up, there's gonna be trouble."

"Get movin' or there's gonna be trouble right now," Powers exclaimed, raising his rifle menacingly.

Bear paid no attention to this threat but continued on with his work.

Trembling with rage, Powers aimed his gun and fired. Bear fell with a slug through his back.

"You'll regret this, Powers," Bear gasped weakly as he started to crawl away. He died before he could reach home.

Powers was at his cabin awaiting arrest when Under-sheriff J. T. Hartup and Deputy L. E. Payne arrived. They took him to Montrose and placed him in the county jail.

News of the killing spread like a prairie fire, and that evening one hundred horsemen rode out of Delta toward Montrose with the intention of breaking into the Montrose County jail and lynching Powers.

The mob assembled across the street from the jail at the year-old Belvedere Hotel—a two-story brick building containing double lobbies, a bar, and fifty rooms.

At this time the town of Montrose had a population of about 300 people—primarily transient miners, cowboys, land speculators, saloon keepers, and gamblers. Most of the businessmen were single, and there was little social life. The few families of culture conducted most of their social activities with the officers and their wives at Fort Crawford, a military post eight miles south of Montrose.[4] The fort

had two regiments of cavalry stationed there, and it was a
small city in itself with all of the modern conveniences and
comforts of life. It was customary for the elite of Montrose
to gather here on weekends for social affairs.[5]

The town government of Montrose was maintained
principally from the licenses of fourteen saloons and dance
halls, all operated on Main Street. The red light district
was in another, segregated part of town. Three stage
coaches carrying passengers and mail arrived and departed
daily from Ouray, Silverton, Telluride, Norwood, Placerville, Rico, Durango, Saguache, and Lake City.

When the lynching party from Delta arrived in Montrose, Sheriff Henry Payne was on his way to Cimarron and
could not be reached. Undersheriff Hartup and the sheriff's brother, Deputy L. E. Payne, who were in charge during the sheriff's absence, felt that protection of the prisoner was too big a job for them under the circumstances.
Consequently, they sought the advice and help of District
Judge John C. Bell, who was a highly respected man in the
community.[6]

Bell, fully realizing the danger, took immediate action.
He appointed and swore in twenty special deputies to help
defend the jail. He refused to let the new deputies carry
firearms, however, since the opposing crowd was armed to
the teeth, and he wanted to avoid a gun battle. He knew
that the side of law and order must make up in strategy
what it lacked in numbers and force.

Fortunately, the mob was so confident of getting their
prey that they took their time, lounging around in the bar
and lobby of the luxurious hotel while making their plans.

Judge Bell knew that it was a race with time. Every minute that the mob could be delayed in its murderous project increased the chances of saving the life of Powers. So, Bell sent five of his deputies over to the Belvedere Hotel to parley with the group and hold them off for as long as possible.

While these deputies made speeches, urging the would-be lynchers to go back to Delta and let the law take its course, Bell sent out other deputies to look around and obtain the fastest team available. After the horses were located, they were hitched to a light buckboard wagon and driven quietly up in back of the jail. Inside, the two jailers were desperately trying to knock a hole in the stone wall through which the prisoner could be removed to the wagon without being seen by the noisy, violent men at the Belvedere.

The rumble of the loud voices across the street grew suddenly louder as the undersheriff opened the door of the jail and rushed in.

"We can't hold them back any longer," he cried. "They're on their way!"

The jailers redoubled their efforts and succeeded in dislodging one of the stones, leaving an opening barely large enough for a man to crawl through.

"Get through there and into that wagon," Undersheriff Hartup shouted above the tumult to the terrified Powers, "or your life won't be worth thirty cents!"

The prisoner wriggled into the narrow hole, tearing his clothes as he struggled out into the cold, night air.

Deputy Sheriff Payne helped him into the buckboard,

The Hon. John C. Bell with greatnephew. Bell served western Colorado as district judge and congressman. *Photo courtesy of Dr. J. H. Humphries.*

and the driver cracked his whip. As the wagon clattered out into the crowded street, some of the mob recognized the prisoner.

"Stop 'em!" voices shouted. "Powers is in that wagon!"

The teamster whirled the buckboard around the corner, heading south toward Fort Crawford, eight miles away, in a frantic effort to reach the protection of the military post. The men in the street were soon in their saddles, and the race was on.

With its headstart, the fast team was able to maintain a slight lead. Shots thundered through the night as the pursuing riders fired at the galloping team in frenzied attempts to stop the wagon and capture their escaping quarry.

After the initial outburst of speed, some of the horses became spent and began lagging behind. Only those horses with the greatest stamina were able to continue the chase all the way to Fort Crawford.

When the lathered, exhausted team finally pounded through the portals of the fort, armed guards rushed forward to see what the commotion was all about. The lynching party—those that were left—pulled up their panting mounts at the gates, not daring to enter. The race for justice had been won.

Powers was confined at Fort Crawford for some time before he was brought back to Montrose to stand trial before Judge Bell—the man who had saved his life.

The jury convicted the prisoner of first-degree murder, and the judge, who had rescued Powers from the angry mob in order to give him a fair trial, paradoxically enough, sentenced him to die on the gallows.

The case was appealed to the United States Supreme Court, where it was reversed and sent back for a new trial. In the second trial Powers was convicted of voluntary manslaughter and sentenced to life imprisonment in the state penitentiary. After serving eight years, he was so near death from old age and ill health that he was pardoned.[7] He died shortly after his release.

Powers' sister, who was not prosecuted, disappeared shortly after the killing and was never again seen in western Colorado.

The abandoned claim on California Mesa was taken up by another early settler. The water dispute had finally come to an end with a total loss to both sides.

FOOTNOTES

[1]Hugo Selig, *Early Recollections of Montrose County*, privately published, Dec. 5, 1939.

[2]Ethel L. Bear, personal interview on phone, 1955.

[3]Billy Smith, personal interview, 1955.

[4]After the Meeker Massacre at the White River Agency in September, 1879, Colonel R. S. MacKenzie at Fort Garland was ordered to move with part of his command to the Uncompahgre Valley to prevent any outbreak in that area. The first troops arrived in the Valley on May 25, 1880. A cantonment, or quarters for troops, was established four miles north of the Indian agency. It was known as the "Military Cantonment" until March 12, 1884, when the name was changed by presidential order to Fort Crawford in memory of Captain Emmet Crawford of the 3rd Infantry, who was killed by the Apaches in Arizona. Although the Uncompahgre Utes were removed from western Colorado in September, 1881, the post

was not abandoned until 1890, after the water squabble between Powers and Bear.

[5]Selig, *op. cit.*

[6]Bell was later elected to the United States House of Representatives on the Populist ticket.

[7]Bear, *op. cit.*

## XIX

# THE BEAVER CREEK KILLINGS

After the Utes were removed from their western Colorado empire in September, 1881, and placed on new reservations in Utah and southwestern Colorado, for a number of years they kept returning to their old domain each fall to hunt. These wandering small bands made great depredations upon the game. They used what meat they could, dried some for future use, and utilized the hides for tepees, clothing, and trading.

The settlers' resentment against this slaughter of deer and elk was intensified by accusations that the Utes were also killing cattle and stealing horses.[1] While reports of their misdeeds were highly exaggerated, feeling ran high, and cowboys from several cattle outfits in southern Colorado agreed to shoot the first Indians that they discovered off their reservation.[2]

One pleasant June day in 1885 a group of cowboys happened across an Indian camp of a dozen or more Southern Utes on Beaver Creek several miles north of the Charles Johnson place, where the village of McPhee now stands. The Indians had written permission from their agent to hunt in that region, and they didn't realize how unwelcome they were. They had stopped at the Johnson store enroute to their camp on Beaver Creek. They were peaceable and minding their own business.[3]

The cowboys assumed that most of the Utes were out hunting so decided to stage a raid early the next morning —Saturday—when all the party was in camp. In the meantime, one of the riders looked over the surrounding country to make certain that no campers were about, since if any of the Utes escaped the planned massacre, they would likely make a revenge attack on any white persons they might find in the vicinity.

When the cowboy returned, he reported that he had seen only one tent in the neighborhood which he said was occupied by a group of surveyors who could look after themselves. The cowboy was wrong in this assumption, however, since the surveyors had moved out the day before, and the Spalding family, consisting of Mr. and Mrs. Spalding and their grown son and daughter, had arrived and set up their tent at the same pleasant location.[4]

Next morning at daybreak the avenging cowboys opened fire on the Ute camp from higher ground. One buck ran out of a tepee holding up a baby to inform the assailants that there were women and children in the camp.[5] The white men shot both down in cold blood and proceeded to slaughter the remaining nine or ten victims, who made no effort to defend themselves.

The Spaldings were awakened by the first shots. Mrs. Spalding called to her daughter, Joanna, and told her that apparently someone was out deer hunting already. Then, volley after volley broke the morning stillness.

Joanna's twenty-seven-year-old brother grabbed the girl and put her on a horse just as she was clad.

"Ride over to that cabin a mile and a half above here," he ordered. "It sounds like an Indian fight is going on, and you must get out of here right away. We'll meet you later."[6]

He asked his mother to get on the other horse, but she refused, saying that she didn't want to make a target of herself.

When Joanna arrived at the cabin, she called out, and three astonished cowboys appeared at the door. When they recovered from their amazement, they invited her to come in.

In a few minutes Mrs. Spalding also rode up, and the two women remained at the cabin until nine o'clock before returning to their tent. While they were at the cabin, the cowboys who had staged the raid arrived. At that time Joanna met Sam Todd, whom she married seven months later.

One Ute miraculously survived the massacre, and on his way back to the reservation, he reported the event to another party of Utes whom he met in the Montezuma Valley.[7]

On Saturday evening of the same day that the Utes were

murdered on Beaver Creek, the Genthner family, who
lived seven miles from Big Bend near Totten's Lake, were
preparing for bed. The three older children were already
in bed upstairs, and the baby lay quietly in the downstairs
bedroom, which his parents occupied. Mr. Genthner, who
during the afternoon had walked all the way to Big Bend
to get the mail, lay fully clothed on the big double bed,
reading the weekly assortment of papers and letters. His
wife, who was in her nightdress, sat nearby reading also.[8]

Noticing a flicker of light outside, Mrs. Genthner
walked to the window to investigate.

"The house is on fire!" she exclaimed.

Genthner jumped from the bed, and grabbing a bucket
of water near the wash basin, he flung open the door and
rushed outside.

Mrs. Genthner heard the report of guns and looked out
the door to discover her husband lying on the ground. As
she rushed over to him, a bullet went through her shoulder. She immediately suspected the presence of Indians,
but none were in sight.

"I'm done for," Genthner gasped. "Go back into the
house and look after the kids."

"I'm shot too."[9]

She ran back into the flaming house where the children
lay asleep. The dog, which also had been shot, accompanied her inside where he fell dead on the floor. She
awakened the youngsters and quickly explained what had
happened. Then, holding the baby in her good arm and
leading the next youngest child with the other hand, she
hurried out the back door, followed by the two older chil-

dren. All of them were barefooted and dressed only in their night clothes.[10]

Their nearest neighbors were William Wooley and his son Doug. Wooley, a Mexican war veteran, was one of the first settlers in the Montezuma Valley, arriving there in 1881.[11] William was away at the time, and Doug, who had seen Indians about the place during the day, had taken his gun and gone out into the brush to sleep.

Mrs. Genthner luckily came upon him there in the brush sound asleep. She had her oldest boy slip up and move his gun out of reach before she awakened him.[12]

Doug Woley told her to lie down so that if any Indians were around they would be less likely to see her. She complied for a while until she became chilled from the blood on her nightgown. Wooley then assisted her and the children to the Louis Simon ranch. When Mrs. Simon first saw the wounded lady, she fainted from fright.[13]

Doug Wooley warned the settlers along the Dolores River about the Indian outbreak, while the Simons took care of the Genthner family.

On the following day some men from Big Bend drove up to Simon's ranch in a wagon to take Mrs. Genthner and her children back with them. Another larger group rode to the Genthner ranch to bury the badly burned remains of the dead man.

Dr. Winters was summoned from Durango to treat Mrs. Genthner's wounded shoulder. While awaiting his arrival, Dan Drake, a veterinarian, came from Cross Canyon to render first aid treatment. At this time it was customary for the people on the Dolores to contribute five or ten dollars apiece in order to give Dr. Winters four hundred dollars a year to come to the Big Bend area whenever needed.

Meanwile, frightened settlers buried their belongings and started for the Charles Johnson ranch at the present site of McPhee. Johnson had a big stone barn with its windows high up along the sides. This barn was located in an open spot where no one could approach without being seen. It was not the first time that ranchers in the area gathered at the Johnson place to defend themselves against an expected attack.[14]

The Johnsons were not at home to greet the incoming pioneers. They were away for the day to attend the funeral of Ben Quick, the first man to be buried in the old cemetery near the present site of Dolores. Quick had been thrown from a horse that he was breaking. He tried to hold on to him and the bronco stepped on his hand. Blood poisoning set in, and although Dr. Winters was sent for, he arrived too late to save his life.

When the Johnsons returned home from the funeral, their yard was full of people cooking and making camp. Some of the women were in the basement of the big fourteen-room adobe brick house cooking tin after tin of biscuits in preparation for a seige.[15]

The neighbors remained there for the next two or three days, sleeping in the yard. No Indians appeared; so the settlers finally returned to their ranches.

When Mrs. Genthner had recovered sufficiently to travel, she went to Durango, where she was met by her brother. He took her and the children back to his home in California.

Doug Wooley, the hero of the day, was an unusual character. When his father William married his second wife, Doug left home and lived alone. He didn't like to associate with people, and if he saw anyone approaching, he would hide in the brush. He became somewhat of a hermit.[16]

After the Genthner affair the Southern Utes were required to have passes whenever they went off their reservation. They were supposed to show these passes to anyone who asked to see them. One day two Indians passed by the Taylor ranch and proudly exhibited their passes.

One of the passes read, "This is a pretty good Indian. He's all right."

On the other pass was written, "This is a damned son of a bitch. Look out for him."[17]

The massacre of the Indians on Beaver Creek was a taboo subject in the early days. Fear of retaliation by the Utes, as well as fear of government action against the killers, played an important part in keeping the subject out of the conversations.[18] Also, none of the settlers, including the participants, were proud of the incident.

The Indian agent at Ignacio went up to the scene of the shooting with a company of soldiers. He threatened to prosecute the guilty cowboys, but nothing was done.[19]

The swollen, fly-blown bodies of the victims lay out on Beaver Creek for a long time. Finally, when the Utes got up enough courage to visit the spot again, they buried the bleached bones of their people.[20]

FOOTNOTES

¹The horse stealing for which the Utes received the credit was done primarily by white rustlers.

²Senator George E. West, "The Oldest Range Man," *Pioneers of the San Juan Country* by Sarah Platt Decker Chapter, D.A.R., Durango, Colorado, 1946, Vol. 2, p. 121.

³Account of H. J. Porter, C.W.A. Interviews, 1933-34, Otero and Montezuma Counties, Vol. 2, p. 358. In possession of State Historical Society of Colorado.

⁴Account of Joanna Spalding Todd, C.W.A. Interviews, 1933-34, Otero and Montezuma Counties, Vol. 2, p. 504.

⁵Account of Mrs. Mary Taylor, C.W.A. Interviews, 1933-34, Otero and Montezuma Counties, Vol. I, p. 101.

⁶Todd, *op. cit.,* p. 505.

⁷Reports differ as to the identity of this survivor. James Hammond of Dolores claims that the survivor was the night herder of the Indians' horses (Account of James Hammond, C.W.A. Interviews, Montezuma County, Vol. 2, p. 497). Mrs. Mary Taylor claimed that the survivor was a squaw (Account of Mrs. Mary Taylor, C.W.A. Interviews, Montezuma County, Vol. I, p. 101).

⁸Account of Mrs. Lucy McConnell, C.W.A. Interviews, 1933-34, Otero and Montezuma Counties, Vol. 2, p. 306.

⁹*Ibid.*

¹⁰*Ibid.,* pp. 306-307.

¹¹Frank Hall, *History of Colorado,* The Blakely Printing Company, 1895, Vol. 4, p. 227.

¹²Account of Sarah Moore, C.W.A. Interviews, 1933-34, Otero and Montezuma Counties, Vol. 2, p. 322.

¹³*Ibid.,* p. 323.

¹⁴Account of Mrs. Howard Porter, C.W.A. Interviews, 1933-34, Otero and Montezuma Counties, Vol. I, p. 175.

¹⁵Account of Sarah Moore, *op. cit.,* p. 321.

[16]Account of Fred H. Taylor, C.W.A. Interviews, 1933-34, Otero and Montezuma Counties, Vol. 2, p. 458.

[17]Account of Mrs. Mary Alverda Estes Taylor, *op. cit.,* p. 102.

[18]Account of Mrs. Howard Porter, *op. cit.,* p. 175.

[19]West, *op. cit.,* pp. 121-122.

[20]Mrs. Howard Porter, *op. cit.*

Chipeta and Ouray. This picture was taken in Washington, D. C., in 1878. *Photo courtesy State Historical Society of Colorado.*

# XX

# THE DEATH OF CHIEF OURAY

On August 14, 1880, Chief Ouray, accompanied by his
wife Chipeta, Chipeta's brother John McCook, and a few
other attendants, left the Uncompahgre Agency, twelve
miles south of the present site of Montrose, and started
for the Southern Ute Agency at Ignacio in southwestern
Colorado. The little group arrived there three days later.[1]

Although comparatively young, Chief Ouray already
had a varied and illustrious career. According to most his-
torians Ouray was born at Taos, New Mexico, in 1833.[2]
His father was a Jicarilla Apache by the name of Guera
Murah, who was adopted into the Ute tribe, and his mother
was a member of the Uncompahgre Ute band.[3]

Ouray once told Major James B. Thompson, agent for
the Denver Utes, that there was no meaning to his name.
He said that "Ooay" was the first word he spoke as a child;
so his parents called him that. The whites corrupted the

word into "Ouray," but his own people, who had difficulty pronouncing the letter "r," called him "Oolay."[4]

Ouray's boyhood was spent among the better class of Mexican ranchers as a sheep herder in the present state of New Mexico.[5] During these formative years he became familiar with the Spanish language. Ouray could talk understandable English, but he had a much better knowledge of Spanish.

At the age of eighteen he gave up his work as a sheep herder and came into western Colorado to become a full-fledged member of the Uncompahgre band of Utes in which his father was a leader. From then until 1860 he lived like a typical wild Indian, hunting, fighting the plains Indians, and visiting the other six Ute bands.

In stature Ouray was about five feet seven inches tall, and he became quite portly in his later years. His head was large and well shaped with regular features. His face, while stern and dignified in repose, lighted up pleasantly when he talked. He had a refined, polished manner and enjoyed meeting and visiting with white men. He ordinarily was clothed in a civilized attire of black broadcloth and usually wore boots instead of moccasins. However, he never cut off his long hair, which hung in two braids on his chest.

While in his early twenties, Ouray married an Uncompahgre Ute maiden, and they had a son. One fall when the baby was about five years old, Ouray and his band went on a buffalo hunt in eastern Colorado. While the men were out hunting, a group of plains Indians raided the Ute camp and kidnapped Ouray's boy. This occurred about twenty-five miles north of Denver.

After his first wife's death, Ouray married another girl of his band by the name of Chipeta. She was sixteen and Ouray twenty-six at the time.

Ouray first came into prominence in 1863 when the federal government negotiated a treaty with the Uncompahgre Utes at Conejos, defining the boundaries of the band's reservation in western Colorado. During the conference Ouray translated the speeches of his people into Spanish from which came the English version through the government interpreter. Because of Ouray's influence and prestige at the council table, the federal government recognized him as the head chief and spokesman of all the seven Ute bands.

Ouray's hold upon his people was always precarious except for the members of his own band—the Uncompahgre band—who were usually loyal to him. He accomplished his objectives primarily through patience, diplomacy, and the strength of his personality rather than by any power that he might have had as head chief of the tribe.

Many of the Ute chiefs were jealous of Ouray's position, and he had many enemies among his own people. The northern Ute chiefs were particularly resentful, believing that the federal government should have chosen one of them as spokesman for the Ute nation, and it took them a long time to accept Ouray.

Even among the Uncompahgre Utes there was some hostility. Once in 1872 at the Los Pinos Agency five subchiefs of this band tried to kill Ouray. The leader of the group was Sapowanero, a brother of Chipeta and Ouray's second in command. The would-be assassins hid in the agency's blacksmith shop as Ouray led his horse across the plaza to get it shod. As he tied his horse to the hitching post, George Hardman, the blacksmith, gave Ouray a warning wink.

The warning came just in time, for seconds later Sapowanero ran out of the shop, brandishing an ax. Ouray jumped behind the post as Sapowanero swung the ax at him, the blow missing the chief's head only by inches. Ouray kept the hitching post between him and his assailant, and when Sapowanero struck again, the ax handle hit the post and broke.

Without the weapon Sapowanero was no match for his powerful brother-in-law. Ouray threw him down into an irrigation ditch that ran past the blacksmith shop. Grasping Sapowanero's throat, Ouray reached for his knife to dispose of the fallen Indian, but Chipeta, who happened to be nearby, pulled the knife from its scabbard just as her husband grabbed for it, thereby saving her brother's life. Seeing how their leader fared, his accomplices in the shop took to their heels.[6]

In spite of this altercation, Sapowanero was usually loyal to Ouray. Whenever Ouray was away from the agency for any length of time, he left Sapowanero in charge.[7] Besides visiting the other Ute bands, Ouray and Chipeta once a year would pack their camping equipment and ride up in the mountains to hunt for a few days.

Ouray backed the Treaty of 1873 which surrendered the San Juan country to the whites. This reopened all of

Chipeta's and Ouray's home near present site of Montrose, Colorado, from 1875 to 1881. *Photo courtesy of State Historical Society of Colorado.*

the old bitterness against Ouray held by many of the Northern Ute and Southern Ute chiefs. When the federal government failed to live up to its obligation under the treaty,
Ouray took a lot of the blame from his people. They
claimed that Ouray and certain government officials were
conspiring to misappropriate the money and annuities
which had been promised the Utes. Some of the Ute chiefs
even proposed to kill Ouray and talked openly of it.[8] However, their plots and smear campaigns failed to overthrow
the great chief, and they finally became reconciled, if not
cordial, to him.

Ouray was forced to kill five rebellious Utes who stren-
uously opposed his policies.[9] This severe method of dealing with his opponents was one of the primary reasons that
he kept his followers so well in line. He understood Indian nature and was capable of dealing with it. If it
hadn't been for Ouray's discipline and influence on the
Utes, there would undoubtedly have been many serious
and bloody outbreaks among his dissatisfied and primitive
people.

The great cross of Ouray's life was the loss of his little
son, who was kidnapped by the plains Indians on a buffalo
hunt. Once it was believed that the boy had been discovered among the Arapahoes. The youth in question was a
young man of about sixteen or seventeen and to all appearances a full-fledged Arapahoe, the members of which tribe
were deadly enemies of the Utes. Out of respect to Ouray
the Indian Commissioner made arrangements to have a
delegation of Arapahoes, including the boy, and a delega-

tion of Utes, including Ouray, meet in his office. There, representatives of the two tribes faced each other.[10]

At this dramatic meeting the Commissioner explained to the youthful Arapahoe, who was known as Friday, that the head chief of the Utes had his son captured a long time ago and that evidence pointed to the probability that Friday was the lost boy.

Speaking through an interpreter, Ouray asked Friday if he could remember his Ute name. Friday answered that the only name he could recall was the one that the Arapahoes had given him.

One of the younger representatives of the Ute delegation told Friday that they were cousins and had played together as children. He informed Friday that his Ute name was "Cotoan."

However, in spite of this reunion, Friday refused to admit that he was a member of the tribe which he had been taught to hate. He returned to his reservation, still believing that he was an Arapahoe.

The purpose of Ouray's visit to the Southern Ute Agency on August 14, 1880, was to induce them to sign the Treaty of 1880. The great chief's arrival was unheralded and even unknown for several hours until Will Burns, one of the interpreters at the agency, by chance obtained the information from one of the Southern Utes. Burns immediately started looking for Ouray's camp and finally found it a few hundred yards north of the agency buildings. Upon entering he found Ouray lying upon some blankets and clothed only in breech-clout, leggings, and moccasins. This was unusual for Ouray, since he usually dressed like a white man.[11]

Noticing that the Indian was restless and in apparent pain, Burns asked him what was the matter. Ouray replied that he had not been feeling well since leaving the Uncompahgre Agency. The interpreter then asked the chief if he wanted the services of a doctor but received no answer.

Burns, nevertheless, went to the agency headquarters and reported what he had seen to Colonel Page, the agent, who, with the agency physician, went immediately to Ouray's tepee. Ouray's stomach was badly swollen, and he seemed to be rapidly growing worse. The doctor diagnosed the trouble as an acute case of kidney trouble—probably Bright's Disease—and he told the agent that Ouray was in a very critical condition. Page sent a courier to get Dr. Hopson of Animas City to consult with the agency physician. A messenger was also sent to the Uncompahgre Agency.

Dr. Hopson visited Ouray twice, the last time being on Sunday, August 22nd. On Sunday evening Dr. Lacy of the Uncompahgre Agency arrived after a hurried trip. While the three doctors tried to treat Ouray, his medicine men were holding incantations and pounding his abdomen with their fists and bucking their heads against his chest to drive out the evil spirit.

From Saturday until Tuesday (August 24, 1880), when he died, Ouray lingered in a comatose state from which he aroused only at long intervals. Late Monday evening it became evident that Ouray could not live many hours,

Buckskin Charlie—a leading chief of the Southern Utes who helped bury Chief Ouray in his secret grave. *Photo courtesy State Historical Society of Colorado.*

and Dr. Hopson returned to Animas City. On Tuesday morning at eleven o'clock an Indian arrived at the agency building and asked to see Dr. Lacy—the physician who had come down from the Uncomphagre Agency. The Indian told the doctor to come at once to see Ouray. They hastened to Ouray's tepee, but before they arrived, an Indian stepped out and silently motioned them back. Ouray was dead.

At the time of his death there were nearly a thousand Indians camped in the vicinity of his tepee. Within ten minutes after he died the Indians had moved more than a mile away because of their superstitious fear of the dead.

Ouray's few attendants sewed up his body in new blankets and buffalo robes and slung it across his saddle horse.

Nathan Price, a Southern Ute, told the faithful little group that his father, Chief Suvata, was buried on the rocky mesa two miles south of Ignacio and suggested that this would be a good place to bury Ouray so that the two chiefs could be together. So, escorted by his wife Chipeta, Chipeta's brother John McCook, a famous Southern Ute chief named Buckskin Charley, and four other Utes, Ouray's body was taken about two miles south of Ignacio and placed in a natural cave on the mesa. His saddle was laid beside him, and the cave was then filled with rocks. The famous chief lay secretly buried here for forty-five years.

F O O T N O T E S

[1]*LaPlata Miner,* September 4, 1880, p. 1. Newspaper in possession of the Western History Dept. of the Denver Public Library.

[2]Frank Hall, *History of Colorado,* Vol. 2, The Blakely Printing Co., 1895, p. 135.

[3]Thomas F. Dawson, "Major Thompson, Chief Ouray, and the Utes," *The Colorado Magazine,* May, 1930, p. 118.

[4]*Ibid.,* p. 121.

[5]Hall, *op. cit.,* pp. 506-513.

[6]Sidney Jocknick, *Early Days on the Western Slope of Colorado,* The Carson-Harper Co., Denver, Colo., 1913, pp. 116-117.

[7]Alonzo Hartman, "Memories and Experiences with the Utes in Colorado," original manuscript copied in masters thesis of John B. Lloyd entitled "The Uncompahgre Utes," Western State College, Mar. 24, 1939, p. 9. In possession of Western History Department of Denver Public Library.

[8]William N. Byers, "History of the Ute Nation," *Rocky Mountain News,* April 16, 1880. Article in U. S. Randall Scrap Book, p. 13. In possession of State Historical Society of Colorado.

[9]Jocknick, *op. cit.,* p. 119.

[10]Ann Woodbury Hafen, "Efforts to Recover the Stolen Son of Chief Ouray," *Colorado Magazine,* Mar., 1939, p. 54.

[11]*LaPlata Miner,* September 4, 1880, p. 1.

Chipeta holding Jim McCook's baby. This picture was taken in Delta by J. D. Nixon about 1912. Chipeta and a group of Utes were enroute from the Ouray resrvation in Utah to visit Buckskin Charlie at Ignacio.

# *XXI*

# LAST DAYS OF CHIPETA

About a year after Ouray's death, Chipeta was moved to the new reservation in northern Utah with the other members of her band. Except for a report in a Denver newspaper on April 1, 1883, that she had remarried a White River Ute named Toomuchagut at the Ouray Agency in Utah,[1] her activities for the next thirty-five years were little known.

When Chipeta first moved to Utah, the federal government promised to build a house for her which would be as well constructed and furnished as her home on the Uncompahgre. Instead, she was given a two-room house on White River that was never plastered or furnished.[2] She used the house very little, if at all, living in a tepee like most of her people.

In 1916 it was called to the attention of the Indian Commissioner that Chipeta was getting old[3] and that she had been sadly neglected by the government for the past thirty-five years since she had left Colorado.[4]

Cato Sells, the Commissioner of Indian Affairs, decided that the government had not shown the proper appreciation for her many services and great distinction as the celebrated wife of Chief Ouray. Desiring to do something for her while there was still time, the Commissioner looked her up.

She was found living with a small group of nomadic Utes who ran a thousand sheep and some thirty cattle. During the summer these Indians pastured their livestock at the head of Bitter Creek near the Book Cliffs in Utah. Each winter they moved their sheep and cattle to a lower elevation in the neighborhood of Dragon, Utah.[5]

The Indian Commissioner asked Chipeta if there was anything that she would like to have the government do for her.

Through an interpreter she replied, "No, I expect to die very soon."

When Chipeta refused help, Cato Sells discussed the matter with the reservation agent, suggesting that perhaps furniture would be an appropriate gift.

The agent explained that Chipeta was an Indian of the old school. She wore a blanket, painted her face, spoke very little English, and preferred to eat and sleep on the ground. During Ouray's lifetime she had lived in a house with furniture, but she had been without such conveniences for so long that she would have no use for them.

The agent said that at various times during her life on the reservation in Utah she had been presented with gifts from white admirers. Almost invariably the gifts had been of such a nature that Chipeta had not known how to make use of them.

Once she had been given some fifty and one hundred dollar bills, but, not realizing their value, she had passed this green paper on to friends. At another time she had been donated a trunk filled with beautiful silk. Chipeta had no need for such finery and gave most of it away. A valuable set of China which had been presented to her was found unused in an old cellar at her summer camp on Bitter Creek, since she much preferred enamel-ware to China-ware.

The agent suggested that a gayly colored shawl would be an appreciated gift. Sells then authorized the agent to spend twenty-five dollars for a shawl. The agent wrote back that the type of gaudy shawl which Chipeta would much prefer was only worth twelve dollars or less.

Since twenty-five dollars had been authorized, Sells decided that the agent should get two highly colored shawls for her during the year. A shawl was then purchased for twelve dollars at the agency's trading store and sent to the Indian Commissioner who, in turn, shipped it back to Chipeta along with a letter of appreciation for her services.

In a short time Sells received the following reply, written with the agent's help:

"Mr. Cato Sells
Indian Commissioner
Washington, D. C.
My friend,

Your beautiful shawl received and was appreciated very much. In token of shawl received am sending you a saddle blanket, also a picture of myself.

I am in good health considering my age and hope to live much longer to show my friendship and appreciation to all the kind white people. I am also glad that there is no more trouble between the Indians and white people, and hope that this state of affairs exists through the rest of my life.

Under separate cover you will find the saddle blanket and hope that same is appreciated as much as the shawl was.

With best wishes I am always
Your friend,
*her mark                                  CHIPETA
Witness:
(Signed)  T. M. McKee, P.M."[6]

As Chipeta grew older, she gradually became totally blind. She was operated on in Grand Junction without success. After she became blind, her relatives stretched a cord from her tepee out into the brush, which she could follow to obtain privacy.

On August 17, 1924, at her summer headquarters on Bitter Creek she died of chronic gastritis at the age of eighty-one. Her relatives buried her in a shallow grave in a little sand wash.[7]

Some time later Albert Reagan searched for the grave while in the Bitter Creek country on government business.

Buckskin Charlie and John McCook, brother of Chipeta, holding bones of Chief Ouray at scene of Ouray's original grave after bones were dug up for reinterment in the Indian cemetery at Ignacio. *Photo by S. F. Stacker, Ignacio, Colorado, in the files of State Historical Society of Colorado.*

Finding it in such an exposed place where the body would be washed away within a few years, the white man advised John McCook, Chipeta's brother, that she be reinterred in a more permanent location.[8]

By 1925 Chipeta's death had become generally known to the whites. When the citizens of Montrose heard of it, a Community Committee was organized to try to have her body brought to Montrose and placed in a memorial mausoleum on her old home site.[9]

McCook gave his consent to have Chipeta's remains removed to Montrose, and the matter was taken up with the Ute Indian Agent, F. A. Gross, who made arrangements for transfer of the body.

On March 3, 1925, C. E. Adams, editor of the Montrose newspaper, received a letter from the agent informing him that Chipeta's body had been exhumed and was ready for shipment. The mausoleum was still incomplete, and Gross wrote Adams that it should be hurried since it would make a bad impression on McCook and other Indians accompanying the body if the remains were put in an undertaking establishment to await completion of the vault.[10]

By return mail Adams wrote:

F. A. Gross, Supt.
Fort Duchesne, Utah
Dear Sir:

   Men at work on tomb. Weather fierce, but we will have it ready.

   Wire when you start or when ready. We want to make the Indians feel we are in earnest and thereby

inspire them to make a diligent search for enough
of Ouray's remains to make a tomb for him (also).
   Better wire.

C. E. Adams
Montrose, Colorado.

The spring was stormy, making the concrete difficult to
pour, and there was danger of it freezing and cracking.
Nevertheless, the work progressed rapidly. On March 7th
Adams sent a telegram to the Duchesne Agency:

"Wire immediately approximate dimensions of Chipeta's box."[11]

The body of Chipeta arrived at Montrose on March
15, 1925. It was accompanied by Hugh Owens, agricultural agent of the Indian service at Fort Duchesne; Rev.
M. J. Hersey, a minister who represented the agent and
who had received Chipeta into the Episcopal Church twen-
ty-seven years before; John McCook, and another Ute by
the name of Yagah.[12]

At 2:30 that afternoon the queen of the Utes was taken
to the Ouray Memorial Park and reburied with an elab-
orate ceremony before 5,000 people.

The Ouray Memorial Park is a historic shrine on the
highway just south of Montrose. It is now owned and
maintained by the State Historical Society. In addition to
Chipeta's tomb, the park contains a cement tepee built
over the spring on Ouray's old farm. The adobe brick
building where Ouray and Chipeta used to live stands a
short distance west of the tepee. It was originally situated one hundred yards north of its present location. This
is all that remains of the Ute buildings in this locality.

North of the building is Chipeta's cement tomb, and beside it is the grave of her brother John McCook, who died in 1937 and was buried there.

The State Historical Society plans to some day construct a museum at the park in which will be gathered relics and other objects pertaining to the Utes' history.

After Chipeta was reburied, the Community Committee of Montrose tried to obtain the remains of Ouray for reinterment beside Chipeta. Chipeta's brother, John McCook, was sent to Ignacio to get the permission of the Southern Utes to remove Ouray's body from its secret resting place.

McCook failed in his mission, but his visit did cause the white residents of Ignacio and the Southern Utes under the leadership of L. M. Wyatt and E. E. McKean, Indian Superintendent, to remove Ouray's remains to the Indian cemetery across the river from the Ignacio Agency.

Four old Utes who had helped in the original burial supervised the removal and acted as pall bearers at the second ceremony. These were Buckskin Charley, Joseph Price, McCook, and Naneese. The ceremony lasted for four days during which time the Indians performed many of their sacred rites. It was concluded by a Christian service.[13]

This reburial of the Utes' most celebrated chieftain was attended by the largest group of whites and Indians ever to assemble on the Southern Ute Reservation.

The authenticity of Ouray's remains was established in affidavits by Buckskin Charley, Joseph Price, John McCook, and Naneese. They were among the six men and

John McCook, brother of Chipeta, standing beside concrete tepee at Ouray National Memorial Park near Montrose. *Photo courtesy of Denver Public Library Western Collection.*

one woman who had buried Ouray forty-five years before.
Buckskin Charley's affidavit reads as follows:

> "After he (Ouray) died, we wrapped the body in new
> blankets and buffalo robes and then tied cords and ropes
> around it and placed it on a horse. After putting the body
> on a horse, Nathan Price, a Southern Ute, told us that
> his father, Chief Suvata, was buried in the rocks about
> two miles south of Ignacio, and this would be a good place
> to bury Ouray, placing the two chiefs together. This I
> agreed to, and so we took the body of Chief Ouray and
> buried it in the rocky cavern below Ignacio in the same
> grave from which I helped to remove his bones a short
> time ago. There were six men and one woman who ac-
> companied us to this . . . resting place. The one woman
> was Chipeta, the wife of Chief Ouray. . . ."[14]

Although Ouray had joined the Methodist Church
about two years before his death, some arguments arose
between the Catholic and Protestant Utes as to which section of the cemetery he should be buried in. The Indian
cemetery was divided by a fence, and it was customary to
bury the Catholics on one side and the Protestants on the
other. The Catholics wanted the great chieftain to lie on
their portion of the cemetery, and the Protestant Indians,
of course, wanted his remains buried on their side. So, in
order to satisfy both factions, the dividing fence was removed, and Ouray's grave was dug half in the Protestant
graveyard and half in the Catholic graveyard.

After the initial enthusiasm was over, the grave was
neglected for a time. The gravestone leaned and cracked,
and weeds flourished. About 1951 a group of public

spirited young Utes cleared off the weeds and straightened the stone.

When Buckskin Charley, famous chief of the Mouache band of Southern Utes, died on May 9, 1936, he was buried beside Ouray. Severo, best known chief of the Capote band of Southern Utes, lies nearby in the Protestant cemetery. He died on March 24, 1913.

Ignacio, most famous chief of the Weeminuche band, which became known as the Ute Mountain Utes, died on December 9, 1913, and was buried in some unknown spot on the Ute Mountain Reservation near Navajo Springs, four miles south of Towaoc. Much later efforts were made to find his body in order to place it near the graves of the three renowned chiefs, but by this time all those familiar with the location of his remains were dead.

The superintendent of the Consolidated Ute Agency supervised a P.W.A. project for the erection of a monument in memory of these four distinguished Indians. The monument when completed in 1939 was eight feet square at the base, five feet square at the top, and eighteen feet high.[15] It stands in the Ute Memorial Park on the east bank of Pine River near the Ignacio agency. Busts of Ouray, Severo, Ignacio, and Buckskin Charley are on the sides of the large memorial as a final tribute to four great chiefs.[16]

FOOTNOTES

[1]*The Denver Republican,* April 1, 1883, p. 8.

[2]Albert Reagan and Wallace Stark, "Chipeta, Queen of the

Utes and Her Equally Illustrious Husband, Noted Chief Ouray," *Utah Historical Quarterly,* July, 1933, p. 106.

[3]73 years old.

[4]Notes on Chipeta by J. Monaghan, C.W.A. Interviews, 1933-34, Moffat County, p. 63. In possession of the State Historical Society of Colorado.

[5]*Ibid.,* pp. 63-68.

[6]*Ibid.*

[7]*Denver Post,* August 18, 1924, p. 1.

[8]Reagan and Stark, *op. cit.,* p. 108.

[9]Mrs. C. W. Wiegel, "The Reburial of Chief Ouray," *Colorado Magazine,* Oct., 1928, pp. 165-166.

[10]Monaghan, *op. cit.,* p. 67.

[11]*Ibid.,* p. 68.

[12]Reagan and Stark, *op. cit.,* p. 108.

[13]Wiegel, *op. cit.,* p. 167.

[14]*Ibid.,* p. 169.

[15]"Monument to Four Ute Chiefs is Dedicated," *The Durango Herald-Democrat,* September 25, 1939.

[16]S. F. Stacher, "Ouray and the Utes," *Colorado Magazine,* April, 1950, p. 140.

# *XXII*

# CONQUEST OF A CANYON

In 1901 E. B. Anderson, a farmer near Delta, ran out of irrigating water during July. Determined to do something about the matter, he, accompanied by J. E. Pelton, J. A. Curtis, M. F. Hovey and W. W. Torrence, started out on September 3rd to make the first attempt to follow the Gunnison River through the dangerous Black Canyon.[1] The purpose of this trip was to ascertain the feasibility of diverting water from the Gunnison to the water-starved farms in the Uncompahgre Valley between Delta and Montrose.

The explorers fitted out two flat-bottomed boats and procured enough provisions to last them for thirty days. They went to Cimarron by train and attended prayer meeting that evening. Then, on the next morning at 10 o'clock they commenced their hazardous journey.[2]

For the first fifty yards of their trip navigation was

good. From then on it became increasingly difficult. The river runners had to shoot rapids, pull their boats over piles of driftwood, and spend much of their time wading in the cold water. On the second day they lost one of their boats and half of their supplies while attempting to run a small waterfall.

Five days went by before observers stationed on the canyon rim were able to discover the whereabouts of the investigators. They had been given up as lost and wire netting was stretched across the lower end of the canyon to pick up the bodies.

The farther the canyon was penetrated, the narrower it became. Banks were few and far between. The water flowed with terrifying rapidity between the high perpendicular walls, which towered above more than 2,000 feet.

At one place the adventurers were confronted with boulders as large as houses, which had fallen into the canyon eons ago, forcing the water to cut out a channel under them. After laboriously dragging their remaining boat over these gigantic rocks, they came to a roaring torrent which moved with Herculean force through a space only 28 feet wide. Faced with this insurmountable obstacle, the explorers finally decided to abandon their expedition after having fought the river for 21 days in traveling 14 weary miles.

Since it was impossible to go back, their only hope of escape was to scale the shear walls of the canyon. On one side was an almost vertical opening in the cliff-like walls. They started up this crevice at about 8 o'clock the next morning, leaving their boat and supplies behind. They

The Black Canyon of the Gunnison measures from 1725 to 2240 feet in depth and 1000 to 3000 feet in width. *Photo courtesy of Benzart, Delta, Colorado.*

First exploration of Black Canyon. Carrying boat over a natural bridge formed by an immense rock slide, causing the water to force its way under the great mass of fallen stone. *Photo courtesy of Walker Art Studio.*

Abandoning the last boat in first excursion thru canyon. *Photo courtesy of Walker Art Studio.*

inched themselves slowly and painfully upward from crag
to crag, not daring to look down into the tremendous void
below. Finally at 9:30 that night they worked themselves
to the summit.

While this expedition did much to interest the public
in the diversion of Gunnison River water, it failed to prove
the practicability of such a project.

Mead Hammond of Paonia was elected to the state
legislature from Delta County on a Gunnison Tunnel platform. True to his campaign pledge, he introduced a bill
which provided for an appropriation to make necessary
surveys and investigations for the construction of this tunnel.

Shortly before this measure was voted on, C. T. Rawalt,
who represented Gunnison County, called Mead aside.
Rawalt had intended to revive the old Gunnison Normal
School bill which requested an appropriation to build a
college in western Colorado at the town of Gunnison.

"Since both of our projects are for the Western Slope,"
Rawalt commented, "the bills may kill each other. There-
fore, if you think that my appropriation will endanger the
passing of your Gunnison Tunnel bill, I won't present it
at this session."

"Would you do that for me?" Mead asked, since he
knew how much the Gunnison Normal School meant to his
colleague.

"Not exactly," replied Rawalt, "but I would do it for
western Colorado. In my opinion, your Gunnison Tunnel
will do more for the Western Slope than my college."

Mead laid a big hand on his friend's shoulder.

"We'll tie our bills together with barbed wire, and they'll either stand or fall together."[3]

Due largely to Mead's tireless efforts, both measures were passed. His appropriation of $25,000 for the tunnel investigation was used up in about a year, proving that such a project was too big a job for the state to handle alone. Nevertheless, a start was made.

In August, 1902, Prof. A. L. Fellows, U. S. district engineer of the newly created Reclamation Service, and W. W. Torrence of Montrose started out in a second attempt to conquer the Black Canyon and establish the feasibility of diverting Gunnison River water to the Uncompahgre Valley.

Their equipment consisted of a rubber boat, rubber bag for a kodak, hunting knives, and two silk life lines 600 feet long. They hoped to accomplish by swimming what the former group had failed to do with boats.

After many days' effort they finally succeeded in reaching the narrow cataract which had forced the other investigators to turn back the year before. The two men, hugging the smooth walls, edged their way forward. They tried to keep out of the swift current, but the violent eddy of water kept beating them against the rocks so mercilessly that they finally decided to swim it.

Professor Fellows was instantly hurled out of sight. Torrence somehow managed to keep his head above water, but for several minutes both men were battered about like corks on a rough sea. Finally, bleeding and exhausted, they reached quieter waters, and they dragged themselves up on a big rock to rest.

After regaining their wind, they plodded onward. They had lost their provisions when swimming the cataract and became famished as the day progressed. Even if they had wanted to quit, there was now no way out of the canyon except forward.

As they were despairing of their fate, two mountain sheep unexpectedly leaped up in front of them. One went bounding up the perpendicular wall of the canyon, where a human could never find a foothold. The other sought shelter between two jutting rocks, which temporarily trapped him.

Torrence reached the opening just as the sheep made a plunge to get out. In its attempt to escape, the frightened animal jumped right into the explorer's arms. After a short struggle Torrence killed the sheep with his knife, and the day's fast was broken.

The next big hurdle proved to be a vast deposit of huge boulders under which the water had cut its way. The rocks were too high to climb over, and the only alternative was to try swimming through the dark, roaring cavern.

With curses they dove into the rushing water which shot them into darkness under the archway. After a seeming eternity the torrent hurtled them out into the open again. With what little strength they had left, they again crawled up on some rocks to rest.

From here on the going was comparatively easy, and it was not long before they emerged from the hitherto unconquered Black Canyon, having traversed its entire length of 30 miles in 10 days.

This remarkable feat accomplished the objective of

proving that the Gunnison Tunnel was a practicable undertaking.

The federal government started work on the tunnel in January, 1905, and its completion was celebrated on Sept. 23, 1909. Water was taken out of the Black Canyon eight miles northeast of Montrose, and the tunnel was 5.8 miles long. It was the second reclamation project completed by the U. S. government in the west and cost over four million dollars.[4]

On Sept. 23, 1909, the Gunnison Tunnel was opened, assuring a water supply from the Gunnison River of 1,000 cubic feet per second for Uncompahgre Valley farms in Montrose and Delta Counties.

William Howard Taft, President of the United States, was present at the opening ceremony in Montrose. It was one of the most impressive events in the entire history of western Colorado.

When the President reached the gates of the fairgrounds in his special car, surrounded by a troop of sheriffs from every county in the state, Charles Moynihan, well-known Montrose lawyer, shouted through the loud-speaker, "The President of the United States is entering the gates. The band will play the national anthem."

The Hon. John C. Bell, who, as a member of the U. S. House of Representatives helped put the project across, was orator of the day and gave the address of welcome.[5]

As President Taft stood on the speaker's platform with the hot sun shining on his bare head, someone in the large crowd yelled, "Let the President put on his hat."

Celebration in Montrose at official opening of Gunnison tunnel. *Photo courtesy of Walker Art Studios.*

President Howard Taft speaking in Montrose at formal opening of Gunnison Tunnel. *Photo courtesy of Walker Art Studios.*

Taft replied, "I wish to thank my good Samaritan friend."

Replacing his hat, he continued, "I am happy to be in this incomparable valley with its unpronounceable name. . . ."

The formidable Black Canyon was conquered and a dream had become a reality.[6]

FOOTNOTES

[1]Barton W. Marsh, *The Uncompahgre Valley and the Gunnison Tunnel,* Marsh and Torrence, Montrose, Colo., 1905, p. 89.

[2]John A. Curtis, "Great Gunnison Tunnel Project," 1922. Newspaper article in possession of Delta Public Library in a scrap book entitled "Delta County History Told by Pioneers."

[3]C. T. Rawalt, personal interview, 1938.

[4]Hugo Selig, *Early Recollections of Montrose, Colorado,* privately published, 1939, p. 16.

[5]Bell was the last congressman to be elected in western Colorado on the Populist ticket.

[6]Black Canyon was proclaimed a National Monument by President Herbert Hoover in 1932.

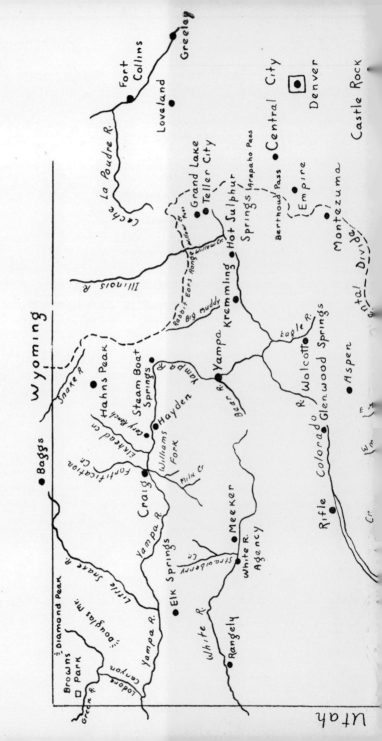